"Did my uncle put me in your charge?"

Trent's maddeningly enigmatic smile appeared again. "Why are you so concerned about my motives for coming? Would you believe I fell madly in love with you at first sight and can't keep away from you?"

"Don't be absurd," Emma answered crossly.

"Well then, I'll have to think up some other reason, won't I?" Trent sighed heavily.

Emma changed the subject. "Tell me about Mexico."

He smiled at her, that dark devilish smile. "Mexico," he said, "should be experienced, rather than talked about. Like love."

"I don't want to talk about love," she snapped, then choked on the highly seasoned soup she was eating.

"Too hot for you?" he mocked, and as she met his innocent gaze with fury in her eyes, he added, "The soup, I mean, of course."

MARJORIE LEWTY
is also the author of these

Harlequin Romances

and this

Harlequin Presents

Many of these titles are available at your local bookseller.

For a free catalogue listing all available Harlequin Romances and Harlequin Presents, send your name and address to:

HARLEQUIN READER SERVICE
1440 South Priest Drive, Tempe, AZ 85281
Canadian address: Stratford, Ontario N5A 6W2

A Girl
Bewitched

by

MARJORIE LEWTY

Harlequin Books

TORONTO • LONDON • LOS ANGELES • AMSTERDAM
SYDNEY • HAMBURG • PARIS • STOCKHOLM • ATHENS • TOKYO

Original hardcover edition published in 1981
by Mills & Boon Limited

ISBN 0-373-02498-3

Harlequin Romance first edition September 1982

CHAPTER ONE

'I'M still not awfully happy about letting you fly back to Heathrow on your own, Emma love.' Joe Kent, marketing manager of Fairley Brothers, of Poole, Dorset, England, shook his grey head worriedly. 'You're sure you'll be O.K.?'

Emma Fairley smiled across the yellow-topped table at him reassuringly. 'Of course I'll be O.K., Joe. Haven't you been training me for the last six weeks, all the way down from Toronto, in the art of Air Travel Without Tears? Airports are home-from-home for me now. Well—almost.'

She waved a hand airily towards the glass partition of the coffee-shop where they were sitting, beyond which the concourse of the vast international airport of Houston, Texas, U.S.A. seethed and chattered and sweltered in the warmth of early April. 'Look,' she giggled, 'what could possibly be homelier than that?'

Joe grinned back, appreciating the joke. In the last six weeks of travelling together he had come to admire Emma Fairley as well as love her—which he had done since she was born, twenty years ago. She had been a tower of strength to him when he got depressed about the business. She could always manage to find a funny side to the worst of setbacks. She was happy to take much of the paper work off his hands, which he admitted was a great relief.

But not least important, she had grown into a beautiful young woman, with her dark gold hair that was always smooth and well cared for, her slender body and long legs, and the way she had of looking at you with a calm seriousness that could change in a moment into that quirky little smile that wrinkled her small,

5

straight nose. Oh yes, Emma Fairley was going to be a great credit to the firm. If, Joe added dismally to himself, there was going to be any firm to be a credit to.

Emma was smiling her quirky little smile now, and looking, perhaps, a little more confident than she was feeling, but she wasn't going to admit that to Joe. He had enough on his mind with the business—or lack of it—without having to bother about her.

She said, 'And anyway, look how easy it's all been made for me! You being a darling and taking most of my luggage on to Mexico with you, so that I'll only have my hand baggage to cope with. And Uncle Edward promising to have someone meet me at Heathrow! So you see—no problem!'

Her tawny brown eyes rested affectionately on Joe's slightly stooping shoulders and thinning sandy hair, and she thought what a dear he was and how she was going to miss him. She said, 'I just wish I could have finished the trip and come with you to Mexico City. I'd been looking forward to that. Nothing but this crazy idea of Lisa's that she wanted to get married all in a wild rush would have dragged me back home before our trip ended. I don't know why she couldn't have waited a week or two longer.'

'Lisa never had to wait for anything she wanted, did she?' Joe's tolerant grin removed any sting of criticism from the words.

Emma sighed. 'I suppose we have spoiled her. She's so very spoilable.'

Lisa, her young cousin—so delicately lovely, like a flower. Lisa, with her lint-fair hair and her dreamy, deep blue eyes. Lisa, so sweet, so loving, so delightfully grateful for anything you did for her. *Had* she been spoiled? No, thought Emma, loving never spoiled anyone.

'I'm glad it's young Richard Southall she's decided on finally, though,' Joe was saying. 'He's a sound lad. I was always a bit afraid Lisa might land herself in some foolish love affair that would come unstuck.'

Emma nodded soberly, marvelling not for the first time at Joe's perception. What would he say if he knew how dangerously close his fears had come to the truth? Her hand rested for a moment on her shoulder-bag, lying beside her on the table. In it were Lisa's letters to prove it.

She changed the subject quickly. 'Joe, I've had an idea. Why don't I persuade Uncle Edward to let me come back after the wedding? If I could manage to get a flight the day after, then I could join you in Mexico City for when the trade fair opens next week.'

Joe shook his sandy head firmly. 'Put that right out of your mind, love. All that travelling—you'd be completely whacked and no use to me at all,' he teased gently. 'And there's no need, my child. I've handled many a trade fair, I can cope with one more.'

'Of course you can,' Emma said, a little too quickly. Not for the world would she let him know that she had noticed how weary he had looked on the flight from New York, and while they had been not very successfully pursuing customers here in Houston. 'But I could help with the letters and the paper work. I *have* helped, haven't I?'

Joe grinned at her. 'Fishing, are we? You know darned well you've helped. You've been invaluable, and it's been a treat having you with me to cheer me up now and again.'

Their eyes met in understanding. Emma said, 'The order book isn't exactly bulging, is it? But everyone says Mexico is *the* up and coming place. I'm sure the luck will change and we'll get lots of new contacts there.'

'Well, you can bet I'll be chasing 'em up.' Joe lifted his thumbs.

She grinned back at him, reflecting the gesture. Whistling in the dark, that was what they were doing. They both knew the score—that the family firm had been slowly going downhill for years and that now nothing less than a miracle could save it. Perhaps, she thought, they were the only two people who did know. Uncle Edward, engrossed in his electronic wizardry, seemed to know little about the business side—and care even less. Or perhaps it was that he was, in some ways, still a child. Geniuses, they said, often were. Lisa took after him in that way; at eighteen she still seemed to live in a world of dreams and imagination.

The tannoy echoed through the room '—passengers for Flight P.A. 317, destination Mexico City, please——'

Joe stood up and tucked his shabby briefcase firmly under his arm. 'That's my final call, I'd better be moving.' He bent to kiss her. 'Take care, my dear, I'll be thinking of you. Wish Lisa all the best for me on Wednesday—and Richard too. Tell her how sorry I am to miss her wedding.'

Emma nodded. 'She'll be sorry too.' But Lisa wouldn't. She'd never even notice that Joe wasn't there. Her lovely young cousin could never understand or share Emma's devotion to Joe Kent, who had worked so loyally for the family firm most of his life. To Lisa, in her dreamy, romantic youthfulness, anyone over the age of forty was already in their dotage.

'Goodbye, Joe, and good luck.' She watched him weave his way between the crowded tables—a thin man, his feet dragging tiredly, and she felt a sudden catch in her throat.

It was difficult to think of Joe as getting old, but she supposed he must be nearly sixty now. He had been part of the family firm, and part of her life, for as long as she could remember and she was very, very fond of him.

When the light aircraft carrying both Emma's parents and Lisa's beautiful young mother to a conference in Italy had crashed over the Alps in a freak storm, ten years ago, it was Joe who had held Emma tightly in his arms, letting her sob out her shock and agony.

Lisa, three years younger, and only just turned seven then, had been almost too young to understand what had happened. Uncle Edward had tried to comfort the two girls, but his own bewildered grief at the loss of his young wife had stunned him, and he had shut himself up in his workroom for days at a time, apparently losing himself among his charts and blueprints and his array of delicate instruments.

But Joe had understood. Had understood, too, that when the first numbing shock had passed Emma wanted to talk about her parents—about her mother, so lively and full of fun, and about her father, who was the dynamo that had kept the family firm throbbing along.

'We'll never replace him.' Joe had shaken his head sadly. 'He had a way with people. He was building up Fairley Brothers into something really big.'

'But you can do it too, Joe. You can go on where Daddy left off.' Emma had felt an odd need to encourage him.

'I'll just have to try my best,' Joe said simply.

Heaven knows he had tried his best, Emma thought now, but it looked as if his best hadn't been enough. She wondered what would happen if the firm really did go bust. Would they lose everything? Their home on the cliff overlooking the sea, in the Dorset village where she had grown up? Would that go too? Thank goodness, she thought fervently, that Lisa had made up her mind to marry Richard at long last—Richard, the boy-next-door, steady, safe. He had loved Lisa since childhood, and he would look after her and protect her from the chill winds that looked like blowing up around the family fortunes.

Emma's face softened as she sat sipping her coffee. Lisa needed someone like Richard. What a mercy she had come to her senses in time about the wild, hectic romance that had started with the Trent Marston man, soon after Emma and Joe had left on their trip! Emma hadn't liked the sound of *him* at all. From Lisa's letters she recognised the type only too well, and she would be eternally glad that Lisa had cut short *that* little romance.

She glanced up at the clock. Her flight wasn't likely to be called yet, so she took out Lisa's letters from her bag. She would read them through once again and then burn them when she reached home. Once she was a married woman Lisa wouldn't want to be reminded of that foolish little fantasy.

The first letter had come soon after Emma and Joe reached Toronto, at the beginning of their trip.

'Darling, darling Emma,' Lisa had written in her schoolgirl scrawl, 'It's happened as I always told you it would! The most wonderful, heavenly man! We met yesterday when he came to see Daddy on some business or other and we only had to *look* at each other!! Oh, Em, wait until you see him, he's absolutely sensational—tall and dark with the most marvellous dark eyes that make my knees go all wobbly when he looks at me. I've dreamed about my man for so long that as soon as I saw him I just *knew*. The blissful thing is that he feels the same about me. Oh, gosh, it's unbelievable to be really in love, I'm just so glad I waited until he came. I want to give him everything and hold nothing back—when *you* fall in love you'll know what I mean. You've always laughed at me for being such a soppy, romantic idiot, haven't you, Em darling, but you see I was right—it *does* happen! I'm sitting in my room looking out over the sea and the sun's setting and I'm waiting for him to come and I'm sort of excited and scared both at once. I guess that's what love means. Goodness, there's the front door bell now and I can hear Jessie coming from the kitchen to open it. I'm all of a shake. Will write again very soon and tell you all the news, Your deliriously happy, Lisa.'

The second letter arrived four days later, as they were leaving Toronto. It was shorter and even more ecstatic.

'Em darling, Just two lines to let you know I'm over the moon, swinging on a star, sliding down a rainbow. All the corny old things, and they're true!! Trent's taking me out to dinner tonight and I'll post this on the way. Trent Marston—even his name's romantic, don't you think? Will write again to reach you in Chicago and tell you all the latest news. Trent's been here every single day. He makes a pretext that it's to see Daddy on business, but of course we both just *know*. Daddy hasn't seen what's going on between us, but he never does notice things. He's working all the time on some new gadget or other and I think Trent means to wait for a bit before we tell him about us, in case Daddy thinks it's all been too quick and I'm too young to know my own mind, but very soon it will have to come out. Must dash now and wash my hair. All my love, Your Lisa.

P.S. It sounds prissy in this day and age, but now I'm so glad I saved myself just for Trent.'

Emma folded the letters and put them back in her bag thoughtfully. The second letter was dated nearly four weeks ago. After that—nothing. She hadn't worried because she and Joe had been moving around and letters could so easily have missed them. Uncle Edward phoned once or twice, but she thought it better not to mention this new man of Lisa's. Lisa had imagined herself in love before, but the man had always turned out to have some flaw—real or imagined. Lisa had always been the romantic, the perfectionist. Everything had to be the very best for Lisa, and Emma hoped (when she went to bed at night and had time to think about it) that this man would turn out to be the right one. But she was inclined to doubt it. She didn't altogether like the sound of Trent Marston, with his expressive dark eyes that made your knees go wobbly. She had met men with that sort of look, and she steered very clear of them.

Then, a week ago, the phone call had come through

from Uncle Edward, when Joe and Emma had arrived in New York.

'Splendid news, my dear,' he had told her. 'Lisa's getting herself married. They've made up their minds very suddenly, and I must say I'm very pleased about it. She says to tell you that you must come home to be her bridesmaid. The wedding's fixed for Wednesday April the fourth, that won't be giving you much time, I'm afraid, but see what you can do. It's a pity about your not being able to finish your trip with Joe, but we can't let even business spoil little Lisa's day, can we?'

Emma had been dumbfounded. Uncle Edward sounding so pleased and placid about Lisa marrying an almost complete stranger at a few weeks' notice!

'But—but——' she had gasped into the phone, 'it's such a surprise—I'd no idea. There'll be all the arrangements to make and Jessie won't be up to that. Couldn't they put it off for a week or two to give me time when I come home? There'll be so much——' Her head had been spinning.

Uncle Edward laughed. 'Lisa's made up her mind on the date and when Lisa makes up her mind nothing will stop her, as you well know. You needn't worry about the arrangements, my dear. Richard's mother has taken on that chore and she's in her element. Lisa spends all her time with her at the store, talking about clothes and so on. I leave 'em to it. She's there now.'

'*Richard*'s mother?' Emma said faintly. 'She's marrying Richard?'

'Yes, of course—who else would she be marrying? And I must say I'm delighted, and between you and me, Emma dear, I'll admit to a certain relief. You know what a dreamer the child's always been, it'll be good for her to settle down early with a sensible young fellow. Now, Emma, will you put me on to Joe. There are one or two things——'

Emma folded the letters thoughtfully and put them back in her bag. She was glad, too, that Lisa was marrying Richard Southall. But a doubt nagged at her and wouldn't be silenced. Why hadn't Lisa written, and why had she let Uncle Edward do the explaining and break the news? It wouldn't be a happy thing if Lisa had decided to marry Richard on the rebound—that was never a good start to a marriage.

Oh dear, she thought, why was everything going so wrong? The near-failure of this trip with Joe, and now the worrying mystery of Lisa's sudden decision to marry Richard, when she had never before shown the least inclination to fall in love with him, as he had always been with her.

Still, she mustn't let herself get negative. Perhaps Lisa would be blissfully happy and perhaps Joe would fill up his order book in Mexico. Perhaps.

Emma put down her coffee beaker and stood up, straightening her slim shoulders, and as she made her way to the news-stand to buy magazines for the journey nobody would have guessed that the long-legged girl in the green suit, her tawny eyes clear and alert, was feeling curiously uneasy about the two most important things in her life.

'England seems so *small* after America,' Emma observed, settling back in the passenger seat as Malcolm, the Fairleys' chauffeur, gardener and odd-job-man steered the family saloon car through London's suburbs in the gathering dusk. 'But I do think it's nice of you to come all this way to meet me.'

The big Scot grinned briefly. 'Och, Miss Emma, it's a pleasure.' Malcolm was a man of few words; his wife Jessie had plenty to spare for both of them. Malcolm and Jessie had been with the family for as long as Emma could remember, coming south reluctantly when they had been persuaded by their doctor that a warmer climate than Aberdeen's would be essential to Malcolm's recovery from a chest injury at work. The young couple had arrived in Dorset with every kind of misgiving and had stayed, all those years, to be happily part of the family.

But Malcolm remained a taciturn Scot and it was quite a speech for him when he glanced aside under bushy brows now and added, 'A man's only in the way at these times, ye know.'

'These times—oh, you mean the wedding tomorrow?'

'Aye, I do that.'

'I suppose Lisa's all excitement? And Jessie too?'

'Aye,' said Malcolm, keeping his gaze fixed ahead.

Emma settled back in her seat and closed her eyes as they joined the motorway. No use trying to find out anything from Malcolm. She would have to wait until she got home to discover exactly how things were.

As the big, powerful car swept steadily and monotonously along the fast lane Emma drifted into a half-sleep full of memories and inevitably they were all about Lisa and their growing up together. Lisa (who was delicate and missed school often) sitting up in their playroom in the tower, scribbling wild romantic stories about knights on great white horses, and noble ladies locked up in castles; Lisa, spending hour upon hour with her dressing-up box, tugging at Emma's hand— 'Come on, Em, I've written a lovely play—I'm the princess and you must be the prince who comes to court me, and Teddy will have to be my grumpy old father.' Later on, Lisa at fourteen, when Emma had been working on Spanish and French for her A levels, had been deep in *Wuthering Heights*, living in that story of passionate love, her enormous blue eyes rapt, her lovely small face ecstatic.

'There must be a perfect lover for every woman,' she had assured Emma in a hushed voice. 'Two people who are fated to meet and be together all their lives. I shall wait for my perfect lover to come along.'

Emma looked down at the book in Lisa's hands. 'Cathy and Heathcliff didn't seem to get much happiness out of it,' she observed practically.

'All right, you can laugh, Em, but I know I'm right. I'm going to wait and I know he'll come.'

'How about Richard Southall?' Emma enquired. 'He's awfully keen on you.'

'Oh, Richard!' Lisa wrinkled her straight little nose. 'He's all right, I suppose, but who wants to marry the manager of a drapery store? I suppose that's what he'll be when he grows up.'

'I wouldn't mind,' said Emma. 'If he was the right man I wouldn't care what he did.'

'Oh, *you*!' Lisa had pouted. 'You just don't understand.'

Emma opened her eyes to the dark motorway, dotted with lights, red and white like a Christmas tree, and smiled a little ruefully to herself. It looked as if Lisa's Great Lover hadn't measured up, after all, and she had had to settle for Richard. Oh well, it was probably a blessing; she only hoped Lisa hadn't minded too much. She couldn't bear to think of Lisa being badly hurt.

It was more than an hour later when the car finally passed through the small village and turned up a steep lane, to pull in between stone gateposts from which the gates had long since disappeared.

The old grey house was a shadowy hulk, lights pouring from every window. As she got out of the car Emma saw the dark shapes of the trees and heard the splash and hiss of waves below, and she felt a happy tug of homecoming.

Then the front door flew open. For a moment the light from the hall outlined a slender figure in dark trews and a fluffy white top, her pale hair lit from behind like a shining nimbus. Then Lisa threw herself into Emma's arms. 'Darling, darling Em, you've managed to get here! Oh, I was so terribly afraid you wouldn't!'

Emma hugged her close. 'Of course I came.' Lisa

felt so small and fragile in her arms. Just a child—too young to be getting married. There was a sudden lump in her throat. They had always been so close—brought closer by tragedy—and Lisa was as dear as a younger sister to her.

They went into the house, arms entwined, and Jessie was standing in the hall, a tall, bony woman in a blue dress, with scraped-back grey hair and kind, shrewd eyes.

Emma kissed her. 'Good to be home again, Jessie.'

'Weel now, Miss Emma, and it's guid to see you.' Although Jessie had long been a friend and equal she still kept to the formal mode of address. 'It's a long trip you've had. You'll be tired, no doubt. A nice cup of tea now, while you're waiting for your supper?'

'Oh, Jessie, that would be heavenly.'

Lisa turned. 'Bring it up to my room, will you, Jessie.' She was pulling Emma towards the stairs. 'I want to show Emma all my things.'

'Och now, Miss Lisa, they can wait a bit. Give your cousin a wee rest.'

'She can have a rest upstairs. Please do as I say, Jessie.' Her tone was imperious. Lisa doing her little princess act, Emma thought, amused.

But Jessie wasn't amused; she stiffened and her brows went up. She ignored Lisa and spoke pointedly to Emma. 'Would ye like something to eat with it, Miss Emma? I'll get on with supper right away now. Your uncle's still down in his workroom. He said he wasn't to be disturbed, but now you're home——'

'Oh, for goodness' sake don't disturb the mad professor, Jessie. I'll see him later.' Emma's eyes met Jessie's, sharing the old family joke, and she saw Jessie relax. 'I don't need anything much to eat, thank you, I had a meal on the plane. Just a couple of biscuits, perhaps. Bang on the gong when it's ready and I'll come down and get it.'

'Ye'll do no such thing,' said Jessie indignantly, and

with a hard look in Lisa's direction she disappeared into the kitchen quarters.

'What was all that about, then?' Emma enquired. 'Have you and Jessie been getting in each other's hair?'

'Oh, she annoys me sometimes. She gets above herself.' Lisa tossed the subject aside, running lightly up the wide staircase with the carved wooden rail.

Emma followed. Lisa wasn't being deliberately sharp and unkind, of course she wasn't. Lisa was never unkind. She was probably practising her new status and authority as a married woman. Lisa had always had acting ability; if she hadn't been delicate she might have taken up the stage as a career. She wouldn't have much difficulty now in turning from the lovely, cossetted, adored daughter to the beautiful, poised, adored wife. Amusement and affection tugged at Emma's heart.

Lisa's bedroom was at the back of the house, overlooking the garden and the sea. She pushed open the door and threw out her hand dramatically, her eyes dancing. 'There—how about that, then?'

Emma drew in a breath. The room looked like a boutique when a new consignment has just arrived. There were exquisite clothes everywhere, hanging from the open doors of the wardrobe, spread on the bed, draped across chairs. Day dresses in jewel colours of fine wool, evening ones that were froths of chiffon and georgette with glittering trims, gay cotton sun-dresses, sleek trousers, sweaters and tops in softest angora and cashmere.

'I'm quite stunned, I can't take it all in.' Emma walked across to where a long dress of softest white satin, the heart-shaped neckline encrusted with tiny pearls, drifted down from a padded hanger. Beside it, on the dressing table, lay a filmy veil with tiny ornaments of pearls and orange-blossom.

Emma touched the dress gently with one finger.

'Gorgeous,' she breathed. 'It really is a dream. London? Paris?'

Lisa perched on the edge of the bed, watching her cousin's reactions with unconcealed delight. 'You're kidding,' she laughed triumphantly. 'It came from Southalls, every last bit of it. Mrs S. would have been mortally offended if I'd shopped anywhere else. She went to Bristol, to some wholesale place she buys from, and came back with a whole van-load of stuff to choose from. I've had such fun. Besides—' she pulled a mock-smug face '—it'll all be good for trade. When the local ladies find I'm shopping at Southalls they'll decide they don't need to go into Bournemouth or London for their clothes after all.'

Emma laughed. 'My word, you're getting quite a keen business head!'

'Well, I'd better, hadn't I?' said Lisa, getting up restlessly and wandering across the room. 'Richard's mother has made him manager of the store, have you heard?' She tweaked the collar of a pink organza dress and stood back to admire the result.

'That's splendid,' said Emma warmly, 'I'm sure he'll make a terrific success of it. I rather fancy being cousin to Mrs Richard Southall. Will you sell me lots of lovely clobber at cost price?'

'As much as you like, you can take your pick,' Lisa cried gaily from the far side of the long room.

Emma felt a weight falling from her. Lisa was really happy about marrying Richard, she really did love him, and it wasn't just on the rebound. No need even to mention those letters or the Trent Marston man—he was well and truly in the past. Perhaps some day Lisa would tell her about that little episode and they would laugh together over it, but until that day came she would try to forget that the letters had ever existed.

She went across the room and hugged Lisa closely. 'Sweetie, I'm so glad about everything for you. It was a bit of a shock when I heard about it, I couldn't quite take it in. It was so awfully sudden.'

If Lisa wanted to say anything about the letters, about Trent Marston, this was her chance. If she didn't, then it proved that the whole thing was just a final adolescent crush, before she grew up and saw where her real happiness lay.

Lisa drew out of her arms. 'Oh, you know me. When I make my mind up that I want to do something I can't wait,' she said lightly. 'And I suddenly found out I *adored* Richard. We're going to have the most wonderful marriage there ever was. Now come and see what I've chosen for your bridesmaid's dress.'

She took Emma's hand and led her to her own bedroom next door, chattering as they went. 'I had to ask Lorna to be the other bridesmaid, of course. She's at the spotty stage, but Mrs S. took it for granted that I would want her. The snag is her hair—she's even more carroty than Richard, when you come to look at her. So I thought it had better be green. It's a bit obvious—green with red hair—but green suits *you* so well, and anyway nobody will be looking at poor Lorna, will they?'

She was giggling as they walked down the corridor, and Emma wished that the silly old superstition about green being unlucky hadn't come into her mind just at that moment.

Half an hour later, while Lisa was talking to Richard on the phone, Emma walked down the garden and ventured to push open the door of Uncle Edward's workshop.

He didn't hear the door open and she could only see the side of his face. His head was bent low over the worktop desk, the spotlight shining down on the thick, untidy fairish hair and glinting on the gold rims of his glasses. A small computer that was his constant companion stood before him, its signals flashing on and off incomprehensibly, and all around lay sheets of paper covered with complicated diagrams.

Very carefully Emma began to close the door again. You didn't disturb Uncle Edward when he was deep in thought and on the track of a new idea. But this time he heard her, and swung round in his swivel chair. 'Emma, my dear, come in.' He began to get up.

She hesitated. 'Won't I be interrupting something?'

He pulled a rueful face. 'I wish I could say that you were—I'm stuck at the moment. What I need is a break, after which all will—I hope—become clear.'

He came towards her, smiling his vague, kindly smile. Edward Fairley was forty-seven and looked older, perhaps because of the deep creases across his forehead and down his cheeks that gave him, Emma always thought, the look of a benevolent bloodhound. That wasn't such a bad picture of him, either, he was always on the track of some new idea.

He kissed her and held her at arm's length, studying her face through the thick lenses of his glasses. 'You're looking peaky,' he said. 'You haven't been overdoing things, rushing about the New World?'

She shook her head, grinning at him. They had a good relationship, and she felt that, in a way, she understood him. 'Nothing that a good night's sleep won't put right.'

Uncle Edward went back to his chair and she perched on a stool beside him. 'Tell me all your news,' he said, but she saw his glance go compulsively back towards the blinking computer.

'*My* news?' Emma hid a smile. 'I should have thought your news here is more important.'

'What—oh, Lisa's wedding.' He pulled himself back to the outside world and its doings. 'Yes,' he said heartily. 'Splendid, isn't it? I'm glad you were able to get back just in time, was it difficult?'

'It was a bit tricky,' she admitted, 'but I managed it.'

He sighed. 'You always manage, my dear Emma, I don't know what we should do without your practical good sense.' He surveyed her with a kind of surprise.

'You're glad—about Lisa?' she prompted.

'Oh yes, very glad indeed. I always hoped she would settle for Richard Southall, but you can never be sure what Lisa will come up with next. Her head's always been in the clouds,' he added with vague fondness.

Emma smiled her quirky smile. 'Like yours, only different clouds.'

'Too true, only too true. I've been a rotten father, I expect. Never managed to concentrate on the job for very long.'

'Don't be silly,' Emma told him warmly, 'you've been the best kind of father—and uncle too. You've given us the freedom to grow up our own way.'

He looked very wry. 'Nice of you to say so, my dear, but I'm not quite convinced it's altogether true. Ah well, I'm handing over the responsibility of Lisa to Richard from now on. She'll be in good hands.'

'And the responsibility for me?' she teased.

He shook his head. 'You've never posed any problem, Emma. I've always been able to trust you to be sensible. And now, from what Joe tells me, you're going to be an asset to the firm.'

She bit her lip, not replying, and he looked up quickly. 'You're worried, aren't you? Things haven't been going too well on the trip, Joe told me on the phone.'

'Oh, don't let's talk business now, Uncle Edward. Leave it until after tomorrow.'

He didn't seem to hear. He picked up a silver pencil and ran it throughtfully between his finger and thumb. At least he said, 'Emma, there's something I'd better tell you, if you don't know already. The firm's going swiftly downhill and if we don't do something about it soon we're sunk. All these years, since your father— left us—it seems that the lifeblood of the company has been draining away. He was the dynamic one. I've always been useless on that side of things, and Joe—

well, Joe's loyal and hardworking, but he isn't your father. And he's getting tired.'

Emma blinked hard. He wasn't telling her anything new, but just hearing him say it brought a huge lump into her throat. 'I know,' she said, not looking at him. 'I thought perhaps you didn't realise; you don't come to the office very often.'

He smiled wearily. 'Oh, I realised. I don't have my nose stuck in a computer all the time, you know.'

'Just most of the time,' she murmured, trying to keep the conversation from becoming too doom-laden on the eve of a family wedding. 'Let's not talk about it just now,' she pleaded.

'There's something I must tell you—warn you about,' he said.

'Warn me?' she asked sharply.

'Yes, I think so, something you may need to adjust to.'

She waited, watching his face, seeing anxiety there. At last he said 'You know how much I value Joe, but I'm afraid the time has come to infuse some new blood into the promotional side of the business, Emma. New blood and new cash too. There will have to be changes.'

'What changes?' she asked quickly. 'If Joe's going to be pushed aside I don't think I could——'

He reached out and patted her hand. 'Ssh, my dear! Listen to what I've got to say.'

'I'm sorry, Uncle Edward, it's just that——'

He nodded. 'Yes, I know. But listen. Joe's getting tired, as I said, and I'm sure he won't be sorry to step down. He's told me so himself. You know, he never really wanted the top job, he took it on to save the situation at a very difficult time. He would have served happily under your father.' He shook his head slowly. 'But there's never been anyone to take your father's place, my dear. Until—perhaps—now.'

Emma caught her breath. 'You're not thinking of

bringing someone in from outside?' She was horrified. 'A *stranger*?'

'I know, Emma, I know. I felt the same way at first. But it's the answer, I'm sure of that. The only answer.'

'You mean you've someone particular in mind?'

He clipped the silver pencil into the pocket of his jacket and patted it. She had never seen him look so confident and pleased with himself.

'It's all settled,' he said. 'I would have liked to bring you in on the decisions, my dear, but it wasn't possible when you were at the other side of the world, and I had to act rather quickly. The bank was getting extremely nasty. So, when the opportunity came I took it.'

He was watching her face closely through his gold-rimmed glasses and his eyes were kind and understanding. 'Now, I can see this has all been a bit of a shock to you. Put it behind you until after the wedding tomorrow, then we can go into it all in detail and I can explain everything. I mean to involve you in all this from the start, Emma. You're a valued part of the firm now and this will affect you personally. I hope you'll be working quite closely with our new director in the future.'

'Who is he? Do I know him?'

'I don't imagine so. He's been away in the Far East and I only met him recently, since you went to Canada. It's all happened very quickly.' He touched her hand almost apologetically. 'He's a first-rate man, Emma. No one will ever take your father's place with me—you know that—but I get the feeling that this man will put the firm back on its feet if anyone can. He has the drive and assurance and personality to do it.'

Emma felt a sudden hot flood of anger and resentment that shook her, down to her toes. Some stranger walking in and taking her father's place! Drive and assurance and personality indeed! She could just imagine him and she hated him already. She had met men like that on the trip with Joe, and drive and assurance and personality seemed to her to add up to push and conceit and arrogance. And she was going to have to accept him and work with him, instead of darling Joe!

Edward Fairley was still watching her face closely. 'Don't make any snap judgment, Emma. Wait until you've met him.'

She smiled crookedly. 'I'll have to, won't I? When do I see Wonder Man? What's his name?'

Much later, she thought perhaps that she had somehow known all along what he would say.

'His name's Marston,' Uncle Edward said. 'Trent Marston.'

Trent Marston—the man Lisa had been crazily, wildly in love with only a couple of weeks ago!

Emma was still staring blankly at Uncle Edward, her head spinning, when he added, 'And you'll probably meet him tomorrow. I told him to come along to the wedding if he could manage it.'

CHAPTER TWO

RICHARD came to supper. Later, he told them, he was going on to a stag party. 'A very mild and respectable one, I assure you all,' he said, his steady grey eyes twinkling round the table under his thatch of fiery red hair. 'Tomorrow I shall be at the church on time, all bright-eyed and bushy-tailed, and *not* suffering from a hangover, cross my heart.'

He turned to Lisa, sitting beside him at the big table in the dining room and smiled adoringly, squeezing her hand.

'Mind you are, then.' Lisa stretched out to the big bowl of fruit and selected a ripe peach. 'I shall wait for no man.' She lifted her chin, acting the little princess.

Lisa had been in one of her fey moods all evening— gay, laughing, brittle, vivacious. Emma, while she was helping Jessie in the kitchen before supper, had had to listen to her gloomy predictions.

'Sing before breakfast, cry before night,' she had quoted, stirring the tomato soup vigorously. 'Miss Lisa's been above herself these last few weeks—up and down, up and down. You never knew what to make of her.'

'Well, at least she'll settle down when she's married,' Emma smiled, wondering if it was true. 'Lisa' and 'settling down' didn't seem to go together.

'Aye, mebbe.' Jessie wasn't convinced either, and her tone suggested strongly that she knew more than she was saying. She had probably been witness to Lisa's brief passion for the Marston man; there wasn't much that escaped Jessie's shrewd eyes. But Emma wasn't asking. She wasn't asking Lisa either. Tomorrow Lisa would be a married woman and the time for girlish confidences would be past. All the same, Emma would dearly have liked to know whether Lisa was aware that Trent Marston was joining the firm and that he would probably turn up at the wedding tomorrow.

Coffee had been served at the table, as Richard had to leave early, and now he looked towards Emma and said, 'I suppose I should be making a move, if you'll excuse me. I'm so glad you managed to get back in time to lend Lisa your moral support, Emma, my young sister would have been very nervous if she had had to take the full bridesmaid's responsibility.' He turned to Edward Fairley. 'It was good of you, sir, to arrange for Emma to come home—I know she was on an important business trip.'

Uncle Edward smiled his vague smile. 'Emma wouldn't have missed the wedding for anything. And I fear the business trip was not turning out all that important, was it, my dear? Markets are not very booming just now.' He had not, apparently, latched on to the fact that Richard had to get away, and now—having been silent through most of the meal—he launched into a long analysis of government policy regarding export markets, most of which, Emma recognised to her amusement, were quotations from Joe.

Richard listened politely and Emma watched him across the table, liking the young man very much. She liked his style—quiet and sincere and straightforward. She even liked his looks; there was something cheerful and appealing about red hair and freckles. She hadn't seen much of him lately—she had been at college in Salisbury and later abroad, putting the finishing touches to her business training by polishing up her French and Spanish, but she remembered him well from schooldays. They had been in the sixth form together. He was a year older than Emma and something of a hero—captain of cricket, champion swimmer, and up with the first three or four on the academic side. A real all-rounder, Richard, and popular with everyone.

She remembered how it had all begun—how he had fallen for Lisa. He had called at the house one day to bring a book he had promised to lend Emma. While they were discussing economics Lisa had walked in; Lisa in palest blue, her silver-gilt hair smooth round her exquisite little face; Lisa at fifteen with her shy, vulnerable beauty. Richard had taken one look and then—it seemed to Emma—had never looked anywhere else.

He's nice, she thought now, really nice. I hope it's going to be all right.

Uncle Edward was still talking. '—I don't know how the ups and downs in the country's economy affects your business, Richard, but we have found it tough going recently, especially on the export side. However—' he glanced happily round the table '—I'm glad to say I think I have found the answer. New blood, Richard, that's what it takes.'

Richard glanced down at his watch, under cover of the table. 'Oh, yes, sir?'

'Yes indeed,' nodded Uncle Edward. 'New blood, and fortunately the very man has turned up. You'll all see him tomorrow, he'll be coming along to the wedding. Lisa, of course, has met him already, haven't you, my dear?'

Emma was watching Lisa, her throat suddenly tight, and she saw the fair head lift like that of a startled animal. There was a look in Lisa's great blue eyes that Emma had never seen there before. A look of naked fear.

Uncle Edward beamed. 'An excellent man, he'll be a real asset to the firm. Marston's the name—Trent Marston. He's been out East, starting up a company for his father recently, and——' He broke off abruptly. 'Why, Lisa my dear, what——'

The peach Lisa was holding fell from her hand. For a moment she stared at her father, her face deadly pale, and then she sagged in her chair and slid sideways.

Richard caught her before she could fall farther. He reacted to the situation immediately, not wasting time on words. He lifted Lisa easily and carried her into the drawing room next door, where he laid her gently on the long sofa. Emma raced upstairs, carried down the duvet from her own bed and tucked it round the still form. Richard knelt beside the sofa, holding Lisa's limp white hand and murmuring reassuringly. 'It's all right, my love, it's all right. You'll be fine in a minute or two. Just take your time.'

Uncle Edward dithered somewhat ineffectively. 'Should we ring for the doctor, do you think? Her heart——'

Richard shook his head. 'I'm sure it won't be necessary, sir. Lisa was very strung up. She'll come round very soon.'

Emma admired him even more. He was a practical young man was Richard. He did what had to be done and he didn't panic or show alarm, or even surprise. Oh yes, he would be very good for Lisa.

Jessie, having heard the commotion, and put her nose round the door to sum up the situation, appeared with a cup of strong steaming tea just as Lisa was opening her eyes, and within a few minutes Lisa was sitting up, sipping her tea, smiling a faint, rueful apology to the little group around her.

'I just got too excited,' she whispered. 'I'll be perfectly okay now, Richard. You go along to your party, they'll be wondering where you've got to.'

He demurred, but she insisted with surprising determination. 'Please go, Richard, there's absolutely no need for you to stay. I shall go straight to bed and Emma will look after me, won't you, Em?' Emma felt sure that she, and only she, saw the pleading in Lisa's great, expressive eyes and caught the note of desperation in her voice.

Finally Richard agreed to leave, having insisted on

carrying Lisa up to her bedroom. Emma waited for him to come down again and said goodnight to him at the front door.

'Don't worry, Richard, I'll look after her and see she gets to the church in time. As she said, she just got a bit over-excited, that's all.' Fervently she wished that *were* all, but she was horribly afraid it wasn't.

She waited until Richard's car had driven away down the drive, then she went back into the drawing room.

Uncle Edward was pouring himself a stiff whisky. He was looking rather pale; he wasn't a man to cope with this sort of crisis. 'Is there anything I can do?' he enquired, wrinkling his brow.

'Not a thing,' Emma assured him cheerfully. 'I'll cope. I'll go up to her now.'

He grinned wryly at her. 'What a comfort you are, Emma. I think I'll go down to my workroom then, and potter around for a while. Come and tell me if I can be of any use.' And to her relief, he departed.

Emma went upstairs and hesitated outside the door of Lisa's room, feeling, for some reason, that she ought to knock before she went in. How absurd—she and Lisa had always rushed in and out of each other's bedrooms without ceremony to exchange news and confidences. She didn't know if Lisa needed—or wanted—help, but Emma had to let her know it was there if she did.

She opened the door and walked in. Lisa was sitting at her dressing-table, staring at her reflection.

Emma walked over to her. 'How are you feeling, love? Better?'

Lisa shrugged, not looking at her. 'Oh, I'm okay. Richard just made a big fuss about nothing. The room was awfully hot.'

There was a strained silence. So it was going to be a cover-up, was it?

Emma said, 'Are you going to bed? Would you like

a drink or anything?'

In the mirror she saw Lisa's mouth twist. 'Tea and sympathy? A nice heart-to-heart chat?'

'If you like,' Emma said steadily.

Lisa got up and walked across the room to where the wedding dress hung, its soft folds gleaming dully in the light from the bedside lamp. 'I don't think I do like, thank you,' she said in a taut, defensive voice. 'I'm a big girl now, I'm going to be a married woman tomorrow. Too late for girlish confidences, don't you think?' Her fingers moved nervously on the satin folds of the dress.

Emma watched her, frowning. Something was very wrong. Love and pity welled up inside her, but she kept her voice low and even as she said, 'Look, Lisa, I've got to say this. I had your letters about this Trent Marston man when I was in Toronto. I saw your face this evening when Uncle Edward mentioned his name.' She paused. 'If you're marrying Richard on the rebound then it's no good for either of you. What I'm saying is that it isn't too late for you to change your mind.'

Lisa spun round, her cheeks flushed. 'Change my mind—what are you talking about? Of course I don't want to change my mind. If you're so interested I can tell you that I realised pretty soon the kind of man Trent Marston is, and that I couldn't feel anything for him but—but—' she hesitated '—but dislike and contempt. He's an absolute bastard!'

Lisa had never indulged in fashionably crude language, and the blunt word, spoken almost viciously, gave Emma quite a shock. Lisa was certainly growing up. But in spite of her vehement denial, there *had* been something between her and this man and he had hurt her badly. Emma's dislike of the unknown Trent Marston deepened.

But it would be foolish to make too much of it. She said lightly, 'There are plenty of that kind around, darling. Any girl can be taken in.' But particularly girls like Lisa—so young for her age, so romantic and heartbreakingly vulnerable.

Lisa's mood changed suddenly. 'Don't let's talk about him. Let's talk about tomorrow. We'll go down to the church first thing. I want you to see the flowers, they're heavenly——'

Trent Marston wasn't mentioned again that night.

'They're jolly late,' complained the second brides-maid, Richard's young sister Lorna. 'I wish they'd hurry up, it's parky here.' She drew back into a corner of the church porch in a vain attempt to get out of the cool breeze that blew straight off the sea. 'Any sign of them?'

Emma put her head outside, looking up the short lane, lined with cars, that led to the church, and the wind slapped a strand of her dark gold hair across her eyes and flipped a panel of sea-green chiffon against her long, slender legs. She drew back quickly. 'Not yet, but they'll be here any moment now.'

She wished she could believe it. She had seen Lisa's ashen face and trembling hands as she fastened the tiny pearl buttons on her white satin gown, not an hour ago. She had held her briefly in her arms as Lisa suddenly gave a gulp and quavered, 'Oh, Em darling, I'm so petrified! I don't know if I can go through with it. Wedding nerves are agony.' She had bathed the great blue eyes and patted astringent lotion round them. She had finally left Lisa with Uncle Edward in the hall of the old house not ten minutes ago, looking like a beautiful frail, misty ghost.

She steadied her anxious breathing now and said again, 'They won't be long. Lisa was a bit dithery.'

'Dithery?' Lorna's rather unfortunately plain little face screwed up contemptuously. 'Good lord, not having second thoughts, is she? It's taken her long enough to make up her mind to marry poor old

Richard. She's not going to leave him standing at the altar, is she?' She began to giggle.

'Shut up, Lorna,' said Emma, with the firmness of three years' seniority. 'Lisa wouldn't do a thing like that.'

'I wouldn't put it past her if she thought there was something better on offer,' said Lorna. 'She's so pretty she thinks she can get away with murder. She was in my form at school, you know, I watched her at it. Ugh, there's a spider here!' She shot out of the corner, brushing her green chiffon skirt in disgust, and dropped her posy of pink rosebuds.

Emma clicked her tongue and glanced through the arched doorway into the church. A wedding between two old local families was an occasion not to be missed, and the small Norman church was full. A discreet murmur of voices mingled with the painstaking Bach that Miss Stevens was coaxing from the wheezy little organ. The scent of freesia and narcissus filled the building and rose in waves up to the ancient roof beams. The five little boys in the front row of the choir stalls fidgeted.

In the front pew she could just see the back of Richard's neck above his stiff white collar and above that the fiery thatch of red hair, neatly slicked down. Beside him showed the fair head of Jim Bolton, his best man, who had been Emma's faithful admirer for some time. In the pew behind, the brim of Mrs Southall's large grey straw hat could be seen to dip as she glanced round with nervous expectation. The two ushers, Richard's younger twin brothers, still stood selfconsciously at their posts near the door, although all the guests must surely be installed by now.

All except one. There was no sign of Trent Marston, thank goodness. Emma would have spotted a stranger immediately. Perhaps he'd decided to give the wedding a miss. Emma had the strong feeling that he was the type of man who amused himself with a girl and then left her flat when it suited him. Perhaps, as he was going to join the family firm, he had a faint conscience about the way he had treated Lisa and had decided to keep out of her way, now that she had found a more chivalrous man. She sent up a silent prayer that he might stay away—a long way away—until Lisa was safely off on her honeymoon.

'Here they are now, I can hear the car,' Lorna's voice squeaked from behind. 'Do I look all right?'

Emma turned back into the porch. 'You look lovely.' She patted a lock of red hair back into place and straightened the pleated green chiffon collar. Then she peeped out into the short cul-de-sac lane, looking for the black family car, proudly driven by Malcolm.

What she saw instead was a silver-grey Bentley coupé. It purred to a halt, double-parking without the slightest hesitation in front of the line of cars already neatly parked. A man emerged from the driving seat and reached back for his grey top hat.

Emma's heart gave an unpleasant lurch and started to beat heavily. Oh yes, this must be Trent Marston—this tall, fabulous-looking man in superbly-fitting morning dress, his ebony-dark hair clustering thickly round his ears, who was walking with the arrogance of the devil himself up the path to the church door, between the two rows of village children and their mothers, lined up to see the fun.

He was inside the porch now and his tall form and masculine virility seemed to fill the tiny space, enclosed between its grey stone walls. Snippets of those letters of Lisa's filtered back into Emma's mind: '—the most marvellous eyes that make my knees go all wobbly when he looks at me——'

Now those dark, slumbrous eyes passed dismissively over Lorna's pink face and red hair and then turned and fixed themselves on Emma.

'I'm late, I think.' The deep, cultured voice contained no hint of apology and the wide, rather sensual mouth no hint of a smile.

Emma felt suddenly hot with anger. Oh yes, he was all she had expected—the kind of man who thought he was God and could do as he pleased with no thought for others. The kind of man she disliked intensely.

'You are indeed,' she replied crisply and with a hint of censure that she made no attempt to disguise.

He went on staring at her and the dark brows rose a fraction. She stared back and as black eyes met tawny ones it was as though lightning flashed, leaving Emma weak and amazed.

The taller of the twins appeared in the doorway, ready to do his stuff. 'Friend of bride or groom, sir?'

'Bride,' said the newcomer, without taking his eyes from Emma's.

When he turned to follow Kenneth it was as if something physical had been wrenched away from her body. She let out a shaky breath. Phew! So that was Trent Marston. No wonder poor little Lisa had been completely bowled over! A dangerous male that, and knowing his own power. A girl would have to be much more experienced than Lisa to recognise the danger.

Her eyes went, as if pulled by some magnetic force, to where he was following Kenneth across the transverse aisle to a seat at the very far side of the church. That was a relief, he was well out of the way there and Lisa could hardly be aware of him when she walked down the centre aisle with her father. And when she was well and truly married to Richard, this Trent Marston would have no further power to hurt her.

Lorna was looking shattered. 'Who was that gorgeous hulk?' she breathed. 'I've never seen him around here before.'

'Nor me,' said Emma briefly. 'I think he must be the man who's going to work for our firm.'

'*Really?* Aren't you the lucky girl?' Lorna rolled her eyes. 'I wouldn't mind working with him. *Any* sort of work,' she giggled meaningly. 'Oh, here they are at last——' as Lisa and her father could be seen getting out of the car, to the accompaniment of 'oohs' from the assembled audience of children outside.

Emma stepped forward as Lisa came into the porch on Uncle Edward's arm, delicately, fragrantly lovely, a dream in white, with a sheaf of white rosebuds, her great blue eyes misty and far-away, everyone's vision of a beautiful bride.

Emma's eyes moved over her lovingly. Nothing to rearrange. Not a single pale-gold hair out of place, not a fold of white satin or a wisp of filmy veil. Richard's engagement ring was on the third finger of her right hand. Everything was in order. She gave Lisa's hand a little squeeze. 'You look wonderful, darling,' she whispered, and Lisa gave her a grave little smile and nodded gently.

Beside her beautiful repose Uncle Edward, unfamiliar in his morning suit, was moving from one foot to another nervously. 'All set?' he muttered.

Lisa made a faint gesture of assent and arranged her arm in her father's. Emma lined Lorna and herself up behind, nodded to Kenneth, who signalled to Miss Stevens. The muted strains of *Here Comes the Bride* stole through the little church.

As they entered, Emma's glance went briefly across the nave to where a man's dark head, towering above the others, could just be glimpsed half hidden by a pillar. Lisa, in her slow progress down the aisle, had passed the spot from where she would be able to see him now. Trent Marston was rapidly passing out of her life.

The little procession reached the chancel rail, where Richard was waiting. As Lisa took her place beside him Emma saw the look of love and devotion on his pleasant, square face and was deeply moved. Lisa was safe now, and if anyone had to cope with the Trent Marstons of this world—the selfish charmers, the callous heartbreakers, it wouldn't be her. Emma stepped forward, took the sheaf of white rosebuds, and went back to her place, her heart swelling with love and relief.

'Dearly beloved——' intoned the vicar.

Lisa's wedding had begun.

The old house was looking its best for the reception. The April afternoon sunshine poured in through the long windows and the big, square hall was festive, with its white-clothed buffet table groaning with sandwiches, canapés, vol-au-vents. The wedding cake stood proudly in the middle, intricately iced and decorated with silver bells. Richard's mother had made all the arrangements and a catering firm from Poole had been hired to take over the food and drink and extra china. Malcolm had brought in masses of spring flowers from the garden and greenhouse and Emma and Jessie had arranged them this morning in bowls and vases round the hall and the dining room, which was being used as an overflow for the guests.

Emma stood by the table, rearranging a small bowl of pink hyacinths, which were already perfectly arranged, and keeping an anxious eye on Lisa, standing beside Richard, with Uncle Edward and Mrs Southall lined up beyond, to receive the guests as they came in.

It was quite ridiculous to feel so horribly jittery, Emma assured herself, Lisa had been warned that Trent Marston would be coming to the wedding; she had had plenty of time to pull herself together before she had to meet him face to face. But as the guests filed in, and the kissing and handshakes and congratulations went on, Emma felt her throat constricting painfully and her fingers digging into her palms. Lisa had been dreadfully upset last night, when she had heard about the Marston man being involved with the family firm, and being invited today. If only she had talked about her feelings, Emma thought now, and not bottled them up! If only she could be sure that there wouldn't be some sort of emotional scene when he put in an appearance!

She had looked for him outside the church, while the photographs were being taken, but he seemed to have disappeared, and the silver-grey car had gone too. Perhaps he had thought better of it, and decided to give the reception a miss? Emma fervently hoped so, but she wished she knew for sure, then she could relax and enjoy things.

The first press of guests had thinned to a trickle when she saw him come in. He stood for a moment in the doorway, looking around, a dark self-assured figure, inches taller than any other man in the room, and making them look as if their morning suits had come straight off the peg, while his had been immaculately tailored in Savile Row.

Emma grabbed a pink hyacinth out of the pot and buried her nose in it, hiding her face while the scent of the flower was overpoweringly sweet in her nostrils. Her eyes were fastened on the group near the door—on Lisa's face as the man approached. It was like a close-up in a film. Everything and everyone in the room went out of focus and she only saw the two of them—Lisa's pale face flushing painfully as her eyes went up to meet the dark, sultry ones of the man standing before her. He spoke, and Lisa smiled brilliantly. Then the man bent to kiss Lisa's cheek and turned to shake Richard's hand. A few words and he had passed on to Mrs Southall and Uncle Edward, while Lisa and Richard were greeting the next guests.

Emma replaced the hyacinth and let out a long breath of relief. It was over and Lisa had been wonderful—calm and dignified. Emma felt a wave of admiration for her young cousin. She had forgotten how good an actress Lisa could be when she chose, and Lisa had risen to a difficult occasion and come through it splendidly. Surely now, she could forget about Trent Marston and be happy with Richard?

'Emma, where are you?' She heard Uncle Edward's voice. 'Ah, there you are. I want you to meet Trent Marston, our new recruit to Fairley Brothers. Trent, this is my niece Emma Fairley.'

Trent Marston held out his hand. 'How do you do, Miss Fairley,' he said formally. There wasn't a vestige of a smile on the hard, handsome face as his sombre black eyes ran over her consideringly.

Involuntarily, Emma moved backwards, away from that insolent, almost hypnotic stare, and collided with one of the waiters, bearing a plate of sandwiches. 'Oh, I'm so sorry.' She smiled at him apologetically, but the smile left her face immediately as she turned back to the man standing before her.

It had all happened in a moment and he was still holding out his hand. It was absurd, but she felt that if he touched her she would scream. She was a straightforward girl, who liked to make her feelings plain. She wasn't the actress that Lisa was, and at this moment she felt a dislike and resentment for the man almost amounting to hate.

But she had to take his hand or risk making a stupid scene, which was unthinkable. 'How do you do, Mr Marston,' she said coolly.

His handclasp was firm and brief. Just for a second her own hand was engulfed in his and she felt the smooth dryness of his skin against her own. She almost snatched her hand away, like a child who has ventured too near the fire.

Uncle Edward beamed on them. 'I'll leave you two to get acquainted, while I go back and do my duty.' He moved away to join Mrs Southall at the end of the receiving line.

Emma stood hemmed in by the crowd of guests—talking, laughing, greeting each other—and wondered how she could get away from Trent Marston. She felt her skin prickling at his nearness. Everyone who passed had a word for her. 'Nice to see you, Emma.' 'Doesn't

Lisa look gorgeous?' 'Hear you've been abroad—was it lovely?' All the time she could see the eyes of the women on the man beside her, hear the unspoken question, Who is he?

It wasn't obligatory to introduce people at weddings and she didn't intend to draw him into the circle if she could help it. She looked around rather desperately for Jim Bolton, the best man. He was supposed to be looking after the chief bridesmaid, surely? But he was dashing in and out with the late arrivals, probably organising the parking outside the house.

Trent Marston leaned down towards her. 'You have nothing to drink, Miss Fairley.' He stopped a passing waiter and took two glasses of champagne from the tray. Just as if he were the host, Emma thought wrathfully, and not a guest—and an unwelcome one from her point of view.

'Shall we make for the verge?' he said. 'This feels rather like the central reservation of the motorway.' He glanced at the guests milling around them and put a hand at her elbow, guiding her towards the double doors into the dining-room, which was comparatively empty.

They paused beside the long polished table where the wedding presents were on display. 'I wanted a word with you, Miss Fairley,' Trent Marston said. He stood very still, looking down at her with that considering look. 'Edward tells me you are a trainee in the marketing department of the firm.' His tone suggested that he intended to end that when he sat in the seat of power.

'I've been travelling in the U.S. with Joe Kent, our marketing manager,' Emma said distantly. She thought it was particularly tactless of him to begin to talk business in the middle of a wedding reception; on the other hand she hadn't the slightest wish to enter into a more personal relationship with this arrogant individual. She disliked every single thing about him.

'I hope you had a successful trip,' he said suavely.

She met his eyes straight. 'It was disastrous,' she said. Perhaps if he really knew the state of the firm he would pull out and go away—out of all their lives.

'I rather gathered that.' The slight smile didn't reach his eyes. 'We'll have to work together to change things, won't we?' He raised his glass. 'To our better business acquaintance, Miss Fairley.'

She gripped the stem of her champagne glass. I must get away, she told herself, before I throw the contents of this glass in his face. Of all the overbearing, insolent *pigs*! She fumed inwardly at the way he subtly underlined the word 'business'.

She couldn't hide her anger now. Her tawny eyes flashed fire as she said, 'This is a wedding, Mr Marston. Sure we should be toasting the bride and groom and not be engaging in a board meeting.' She glanced through into the hall. 'Everyone has arrived now, I think they'll be cutting the cake any moment. Please excuse me.'

She put her untasted glass of champagne down and swept out of the room, her dark gold head held high, the filmy green dress swishing round her pretty legs, the heels of her silver shoes clicking smartly on the polished wood floor.

It was as well that he should recognise her hostility from the beginning, she told herself, then they would know exactly where they stood with each other.

She just wished she could have made her point without ending up by shaking as if she had a high fever, and feeling slightly sick. And she wished even more that, although she had her back to him, she did not feel those dark, sleepy eyes following her as she went.

As she crossed the hall she saw Jim Bolton, the best man, weaving his way towards her.

'Emma, sweet, forgive me, I should have been looking after you. The best man's the dogsbody around here—the jobs they find me to do!' He ogled her shamelessly. 'You look superb, lovey. Like a naiad or a dryad or something.' He had obviously been drinking to soothe his nerves even before the wedding began. 'I'll look after you now, though. Claim best man's privilege f'r a start.' Before she knew what he intended to do he had put both arms round her and kissed her— a kiss that was a little too enthusiastic and went on a little too long for the occasion.

Emma drew back. 'Hey, that's enough! And I thought the best man's privilege was to kiss the bride.'

He kept one arm tightly round her. 'Rather kiss you, Emma sweet, You're one hundred per cent more sexy.'

'You've been drinking too much,' she said severely, wriggling out of his grasp. But she smiled up into his fair, good-looking face. They had been friends for years and he proposed to her regularly, without much hope.

'Aw, what 'r weddings for?' he chuckled. 'Free drinks and free kisses.'

With a small shock Emma realised that a tall figure was standing quite close, watching the performance with interest. Trent Marston must have followed her, damn him!

She turned her back on him and encountered Mrs Southall, elegant in a silver-grey suit, and made up immaculately. 'My dear Emma, how charming you look!'

Mrs Southall was a tall, commanding woman who had managed the large store in the nearby holiday town since the death of her husband. She was in her element now, playing hostess at the wedding of her son.

'I wanted a word with you, my dear.' The grey hat dipped towards Emma confidentially. 'I do so hope you don't think I've been interfering, in making all the wedding arrangements. Of course, we realised that it should have been your job, but as it was all decided so quickly and as you weren't here——'

'Oh, please, Mrs Southall, don't think of it like that. You've done it all superbly—much better than I could have done, and Lisa's very grateful.'

Mrs Southall beamed. 'Thank you, my dear.' She looked towards Lisa and Richard. 'Don't they make a lovely couple? Lisa is so beautiful and such a sweet girl. I'm sure they'll be wonderfully happy.' She sighed gustily. 'She will be a great asset to Richard at the store. She pays for dressing, as my mother used to say. Ah, they're going to cut the cake, I see, we must gather round. I shall see you this evening at my little party?'

'Thank you, Mrs Southall.' Emma did not feel in a party-going mood, but it would have been unkind to refuse.

'Just for the young people, you know. An informal supper and some dancing.' She looked round as if she were searching for someone. 'Ah, there you are, Mr Marston, I've been looking for you.' She placed a retaining hand on his sleeve and smiled up glowingly into his eyes. 'I'm giving a small party this evening at my house—I shall be so delighted if you will come along. You could perhaps bring Emma, as you're staying with Mr Fairley.'

'Oh, but——' Emma began. She hadn't realised that Uncle Edward had invited the Marston individual to stay overnight. Jessie must have prepared a room for him and forgotten to mention it. Her heart sank. She had been banking on his leaving after the reception, and the prospect of having him around filled her with something very like panic.

'Thank you, Mrs Southall, I shall be delighted, and I'll have great pleasure in giving Emma a lift.' Trent Marston was saying courteously.

'Splendid, we'll look forward to seeing you.' Mrs Southall was known as a hardheaded business woman, but now she was in quite a flutter, Emma thought disgustedly. This man just had to look at a woman with those dark, mocking eyes of his to have her purring like a bemused kitten. He was pure dynamite, no doubt about that. Her own heart had given a quick lurch as he had spoken her name just now, and it wouldn't do at all.

As Mrs Southall turned towards the group round the buffet table she said in a low voice, 'Thank you, but I expect Jim will be calling for me.'

The dark eyebrows went up a fraction. 'Jim? Is that the best man? The one who was wallowing in free kisses just recently?' He glanced across the hall. 'He'll need to sober up before he gives anyone a lift anywhere.'

She turned on him angrily, but he had moved away and there was nothing she could do but fume impotently. She moved across to stand beside Jim while the cake-cutting ceremony and the speeches went on. In a kind of daze she heard the clapping, saw the cameras flash. Uncle Edward's speech was short, Richard's even shorter, and they both looked very glad when the ordeal was over. When Jim came to propose the bridesmaids he was inclined to ramble on in a slightly maudlin voice, an arm round each girl. He *was* rather drunk, Emma had to admit—that odious Trent Marston was right. She disliked him even more.

The reception pursued the course of all receptions. The talk and laughter increased as the buffet table and champagne bottles emptied. Emma was drawn into one chattering group after another. Jim Bolton was no support at all. He had found himself a chair in the dining room and slumped into it, looking happy and stupid and willing to chat to anyone who passed, but unwilling to get up and circulate. Emma was annoyed with him; she had depended on him to stay beside her and insulate her from any further contact with Trent Marston. As it was she had to keep an eye on him and move out of the way if he seemed to be getting near.

She kept an eye on Lisa too. This was Lisa's day and she was carrying it off magnificently, always the

centre of an admiring group, lavish with their compliments and praise. Richard never moved from her side.
He looked the picture of happiness and his hand
reached constantly for hers, his arm went round her
shoulder as if he couldn't bear to be separated from his
new wife. They were the perfect, blissfully happy
newlyweds, Emma assured herself. So what had she
been worrying about?

She glanced at her watch. In ten minutes or so she
must contact Lisa and take her upstairs to change into
her going-away outfit. She and Richard were to drive
into Poole and catch the London train, staying there
overnight, ready to fly to the Seychelles tomorrow
morning.

For a moment Emma found herself alone. The swell
of talk had died down a little. One or two of the women
were looking pink and slightly exhausted. Lorna was
giggling away with two young men—friends of her
brothers—and having a high old time. Uncle Edward
was nowhere to be seen. Emma grinned to herself as
she thought that he had probably sloped off to his
study, which was conveniently along the passage that
led to the kitchens and the back stairs. He had coped
splendidly, but social occasions were definitely not his
cup of tea. She would go and have a quick word with
him and then look in upon Jessie, who was queening it
over the hired waiters in the kitchen. Jessie had
attended the ceremony, in her best lilac-coloured dress
and coat, but nothing would persuade her to mix with
the guests at the reception.

'Malcolm and me will be happiest in the kitchen,
Miss Emma,' she had decreed, and could not be shifted
from that decision.

Emma took a quick look round to check that she
wouldn't encounter Trent Marston, but couldn't see
him, so she stepped purposefully across the hall, under
the archway and down the long passage.

It was as she reached the corner by the window

alcove that she heard the study door open and some inner warning made her stop dead as a deep, hatefully familiar voice said, 'Good, that's splendid. Then we'll discuss it later, shall we, Edward? Tonight, perhaps, when I get back from this party?'

The door closed. Footsteps approached.

It was a stupid thing to do, a blind impulse, but Emma wasn't in a mood to stop and consider. All she wanted at that moment was to avoid meeting the man and having to speak to him. She stepped into the alcove, behind the long red velvet curtain. The footsteps approached and she held her breath. Then there was a rush and a rustle passing the alcove from the opposite direction and she caught a glimpse of white satin.

Lisa's voice, trembling and breathless, came clearly. 'Trent, I had to find you—to speak to you. Why did you come? Why couldn't you have stayed away from my wedding?' The words were spilling out, agonised, pleading.

'My dear girl, why shouldn't I ome?' He barely troubled to hide his impatience. 'I was invited.'

'Not by me. I just prayed and prayed that I'd never see you again in my life. After the way you treated me——'

'Oh, for God's sake don't start all that again!' He sounded harsh, utterly without feeling. 'I've had quite enough of that sort of talk. You're married now, to a decent man. Why don't you grow up, Lisa?'

'Grow up—is that all you can say? Grow up?' Her voice rose hysterically. 'After all we were to each other? I loved you—loved you as I've never loved any other man and never will——' She was almost screaming now.

Trent Marston's reply came low and vicious. 'Shut up, you stupid little fool, and pull yourself together! Just take it that I don't love you, never did. Anything that happened was your idea, your choice, not mine. I don't give a damn for you, Lisa, just remember that. Now go back to your husband and stop behaving like a spoilt child!'

There was a gasp, a strangled sob, and then Lisa's footsteps stumbled away along the passage towards the back stairs. After that there was silence.

Emma's hand clutched the curtain. She was cold with shock, her knees were shaking. At that moment she had no power over her body at all and even if she had tried, she lacked the control to stay squeezed behind the curtain. She stood there waiting for Trent Marston to reach the window and see her.

He got to the spot where she stood, and stopped dead, his dark eyes sweeping over her in a long, raking look, taking in the situation immediately. She squirmed inside, hanging on to the red velvet curtain like some guilty woman in a French farce.

His sensual mouth twisted. 'Well, well, doing a little snooping, were you, Miss Fairley? I trust you were rewarded, but I assure you that I didn't seek that spot of melodrama.'

His tone was withering, but rage and resentment steadied her, stiffening her muscles so that she was able to stand straight and meet his hard, contemptuous gaze.

'And I certainly didn't seek to witness it.' She was pleased that her voice was reasonably steady although her throat was achingly tight. 'I was merely taking evasive action to avoid meeting you.' She raised her chin a fraction. 'I find it difficult to be polite to you, Mr Marston.'

'Really?' The thick black brows rose a fraction. 'Then why try?'

'This happens to be my home. And the occasion should be a happy one.'

The small smile didn't reach his eyes. 'Your cousin seems to think otherwise.'

'My cousin is very young and very vulnerable,' she

retorted, breathing quickly. 'She may have been foolish enough to imagine herself in love with you, but did you have to be so disgustingly brutal?'

'It was necessary to spell it out. Your cousin is a leech, Miss Fairley. She would cling on to a man with those pretty white teeth. A man must protect himself. If you call that being disgustingly brutal, so be it.' He shrugged indifferently and half turned to move away.

Emma's cool deserted her finally. The blood ran hotly into her cheeks, her tawny eyes flashed golden fire, her hands clenched. 'Oh——' she spat out '—I think you're the most odious—hateful—despicable man I've ever met! I'd like to——' Her hand went up automatically to strike out at the hard, arrogant face above her, but he caught her wrist and held it in a grip that made her wince.

'Oh no, you don't, Miss Fairley. This is no business of yours.' His voice was icy. 'Your cousin is a married woman and has a man to rush to her defence if she thinks it necessary.'

He loosened his grip and tossed her hand aside contemptuously. His eyes sent shivers down her spine. 'Two hysterical females are altogether too much for one afternoon. Please excuse me.'

He turned away and strode down the passage and disappeared from sight.

CHAPTER THREE

SHAKING with wrath and humiliation, Emma stood staring at the spot where Trent Marston had disappeared. Her wrist hurt where he had grasped it and she rubbed it fretfully, as if she could rub away the feeling of his skin touching hers. She wanted to rush up to her room and thump the pillows to work off the helpless frustration she felt.

But there was Lisa to be thought of. Emma turned round and walked slowly up the back stairs. Lisa would get over it in time, of course she would, but it would do no good to tell her that now. After hearing that passionate outburst she didn't know what to expect when she saw Lisa, but whatever it was, she had to calm her down. Somehow Lisa had to change into her going-away clothes; somehow she had to smile and wave through all the ritual of the confetti-throwing, the 'Just Married' signs on the car, and any other wedding jokes that Richard's young brothers were no doubt planning. Somehow she had to climb into that car looking blissful, and be whisked away to a life that was empty of the man she loved. That was quite a challenge for any eighteen-year-old girl, but for sensitive, vulnerable Lisa it could be desperate.

Lisa was standing motionless in the middle of her bedroom. As Emma opened the door she spun round, her eyes blazing.

'You heard, didn't you? You were hiding behind that curtain, spying on me. I saw your dress as I ran past, but I was too worked up to stop then. That was a dirty trick, Em, I wouldn't have believed it of you!'

Emma went further into the room. 'Now, wait a minute, love, I was *not* spying on you. You know per-

48

fectly well I wouldn't spy on you. I'd slipped in there
to avoid that awful Marston man when you came hare-
ing past. There wasn't a thing I could do. But I'm
sorry I had to hear—if you want, I'll forget every
word.'

Lisa stared blankly at her, then, very slowly, her
great blue eyes filled with tears and she slid down on
to the bed. 'It doesn't matter,' she gulped. 'Oh, Em,
I'm sorry. Of course you wouldn't spy on me. It's just
that I—I'm so shattered. He has such an awful effect
on me.'

Emma thrust a handkerchief into her hand and she
wiped her eyes and blew her nose and rushed on,
choking a little. 'Oh, I hate him—I loathe him! But I
only had to see him—to hear his voice——' She began
to cry again, then pulled herself together with a visible
effort. 'All I wanted was to forget him. When he went
away I thought I'd never see him again. And now he's
going to be around here all the time—part of the firm.
He'll come to the house. *You'll* be working with him,
Em, travelling abroad with him——'

'I certainly will not,' Emma broke in firmly. 'Not on
your life! I've met men like him and I keep well away
from them. No, don't worry about me, I'm quite capable of taking avoiding action. Anyway, he'll most
likely be based in London, so I shan't see anything of
him.'

Lisa stopped crying. 'Do you really think so?'

'Yes, I do.' Emma sensed a breakthrough and began
to build on it. 'Look, love, I know it's damnably difficult, but you've got to put all this behind you. You're
married to Richard and he's a dear and he adores you.
You're the sun and the moon and all the stars to him,
and when you go down you're going to look radiant.
Everyone down there is crazy about you—the way you
look, the way you behave. Such dignity! Such poise!
Mrs Southall said you were just like the young Princess
Grace.' She hadn't, but Emma was sure she would

have done if she'd thought of it.

Lisa produced a watery little smile. 'Did she really?'

'And poor Lorna is consumed with jealousy,' Emma pressed on, hoping she wasn't overdoing it. 'She knows she hasn't much hope of getting a husband herself, poor child. She's rather plain, isn't she?'

'Yes, I *am* the first of my form to get married.' Lisa's huge eyes took on the faintest of sparkles. She fingered the skirt of the going-away outfit, laid out on the bed beside her. 'It's pretty, don't you think, Em?' she said wistfully.

The suit of softest cotton corduroy, in a delicate powdery blue with an antique silver clasp on the belt, was a smash hit and Emma said so, and went on saying so while she helped Lisa to slip out of the wedding gown and repair her make-up. By the time she was dressed and ready to go downstairs, Lisa was giving a very convincing performance of a radiant bride leaving on her honeymoon. There was just one more hurdle left to cross and Emma kept tight hold of Lisa's hand, her eyes passing anxiously over the crowd of guests for a dark head towering above all the rest. But Trent Marston was nowhere to be seen, and she breathed easily again.

Richard was waiting at the top of the steps outside the front door. He had changed too and he looked very spruce in his casual grey suit. He came forward eagerly as Lisa and Emma appeared, which was a signal for the twins and their two friends to produce guitars from somewhere and launch themselves into a somewhat ribald song which might have gone down well in a men's club but was certainly out of place at a quiet, conventional wedding in a country village.

Lisa glanced at the singers and turned away, flushing, and Richard glowered fiercely at the boys. 'That's enough of that. Pack it in—it's in bloody bad taste.'

He spoke in a low, warning voice, but Emma was standing near and heard every word. It seemed, she thought wryly, that she was destined today to overhear embarrassing exchanges.

Kenneth, the taller of the twins, looked sulky. 'For Pete's sake, Rick, can't you take a joke?'

Richard glanced at Lisa. 'Just *stop* it, will you, Ken? Lisa doesn't go for that sort of song.'

Kenneth pulled a face and obeyed, signing to the others. The music stopped. Richard moved nearer to Lisa and put a protective arm around her and murmured something in her ear.

Emma was quite impressed. She hadn't known that Richard could be so authoritative and she admired him all the more for it. He was right, too. The song was decidedly off colour for a wedding like this.

Lisa was saying her goodbyes now. She came to Emma last and put her arms around her. 'Goodbye, Em darling, you've been wonderful to me always and I love you so much.' The great blue eyes were misty. 'I *trust* you, you know that, don't you?'

She put her hand in Richard's and they ran down the steps and into the car. Showers of confetti followed them and they ducked and laughed. A moment later they were on their way, waving through the windows as they rounded the corner of the drive.

The usual anti-climax descended on the wedding party, a slackening of tension now the married couple had left. Emma's tension slackened too and she breathed a sigh of profound relief that Trent Marston had had the decency to keep away from the seeing-off ceremony. Except, of course, that it wasn't decency that had motivated him but something entirely selfish. He had already shown himself as the kind of man who will amuse himself with a girl and then toss her aside quite callously. Emma seethed inside again, remembering his brutal words to Lisa in the passage outside the study.

Uncle Edward approached, looking exhausted and relieved. 'Well, that all seemed to go off fairly well, don't you think?'

'Splendidly,' agreed Emma. 'Wasn't she lovely?'

He nodded slowly. 'So like her mother.' His eyes met Emma's 'If only——' he added in a low voice, and she squeezed his hand, understanding.

Emma waited until the final car had driven away and then she went out to the kitchen to congratulate Jessie on her part in the festivities. The hired waiters had packed up and departed in the van, with their crates of china and glass and a good box of perks in the shape of left-overs, Jessie informed her. 'They were guid boys, they did well. I let them have a bottle of beer each, I hope Mr Edward will no' mind?'

'Of course not.' Emma sank into the basket chair opposite Jessie's, heaving a sigh. 'It was a lovely wedding and everything went splendidly. Lisa's lucky, don't you think, Jessie? Richard's a really nice boy.'

'Oh aye,' said Jessie. She folded her hands on her apron. 'Miss Lisa did the sensible thing for once. When she could'na get the one she wanted she took the next best one. I've not known her do that before,' she added.

Emma was used to Jessie's plain speaking. Like an old family nurse, she had the privilege of saying what she thought.

'You mean she had a crush on this Marston man?' Emma smiled, making it sound trivial. 'She mentioned him in her letters.'

'Did she now?' Jessie said darkly. 'I wonder what she told you?'

'Not much, really.' Emma stood up. She wasn't going to discuss Lisa with Jessie. It would seem like disloyalty. 'I'd better go up and get changed. Mrs Southall's giving a party this evening and there'll be lots of food, so don't bother about any supper for me, Jessie.'

Jessie pulled herself to her feet, a little wearily. 'I'll be taking off my finery too.' She brushed down the

skirt of the lilac dress and the shrewd eyes twinkled.
I'll be needing it again when you get married, Miss
Emma.'

'Me? Oh, I shan't be getting married for ages yet.
I'm choosy.' She helped herself to a tiny sausage roll
from a plate of left-overs, suddenly realising that she
was hungry. She had been far too tense during the
reception to eat anything. 'Um, these are good. No,
I'm going to be busy working for the firm. I learned a
lot from Joe on our trip.'

Jessie carried her empty tea-cup to the sink. 'Aye,
Joe's a guid man, but he's getting on a bit now. You'll
be working with this Mr Marston, then?'

Oh lord, here it was again! Couldn't she be allowed
to forget the man for a moment?

'I really don't know,' she said vaguely, turning to the
door.

Jessie looked over her shoulder. 'Miss Lisa won't
take kindly to it if you do,' she said flatly.

Emma couldn't let that go. 'Lisa? Why should she
mind? She's married now.'

'Oh aye, she's married, but she's still just a child.
She would'na like you getting together with Mr
Marston, I can tell you that.'

'Getting together?' Emma almost exploded. 'What
do you mean, Jessie?'

Jessie didn't smile often, but sometimes her face took
on a wry, mischievous look, as it did now. 'Och, I don't
mean anything, except that you'd make a bonny pair,
the two of you.'

It was no good getting angry with Jessie. Evidently
the Marston individual had been working on her, too,
with his lazy dark eyes and his machismo. Better make
it into a joke. It was quite an effort, but she managed
to laugh. 'You'd better watch that imagination of
yours, Jessie. I hardly know the man.' She couldn't
resist adding, '—and I don't at all like what I do
know.'

Jessie raised scanty eyebrows. 'Oh, aye?' she said, and turned back to the sink.

Outside the kitchen door Emma stood looking up and down the passage, wondering where Trent Marston was, almost holding her breath. Then she pulled herself together. She would have to encounter the man again at some time, so it was quite ridiculous to behave like some silly heroine in an adventure film, hiding behind curtains, peering round corners. She tossed back her head and marched towards the back staircase.

'Miss Fairley——' A deep voice from behind brought her up sharply with a twinge of something that felt like fear at the pit of her stomach.

'Yes?' she said, raising her eyebrows faintly.

He stood in the study doorway, one hand on the door-knob, evidently intending to go back inside. He must have been listening for her, recognising her step on the tiled floor. 'I wondered when you would like to leave for the party,' he said. 'I'm at your service, any time.'

Pompous beast, she thought. At my service indeed—that's a lie!

'I won't need to trouble you, Mr Marston,' she said coolly, avoiding his eyes. But it was almost worse to focus on the long length of his body in its well-fitting formal suit as he leaned nonchalantly against the doorpost, and imagine herself sitting beside him in the intimate closeness of his car. No, she *couldn't*!

Uncle Edward appeared behind Trent in the doorway. 'Aren't you going to the party, Emma? You're all right, are you, my dear? Not ailing? Not suffering from jet-lag?'

'No, I'm fine.' She smiled brilliantly at him. 'It's just that I'm not sure how long I'll be, so I won't bother Mr Marston. When I'm ready Malcolm can give me a lift. Or I could drive myself if the Mini's O.K.'

'No need, my dear, no need at all,' Uncle Edward assured her. 'Malcolm has taken the lad from the garage into Poole, to drive Richard's car back. And I'm afraid your Mini has gone in for servicing and re-spraying. I thought it would be a little surprise for you, when you got home.'

'Oh,' said Emma rather blankly. 'That's a lovely sur-prise—and how good of you to think of it.'

Edward smiled. 'As a matter of fact, my dear, I must admit that it was Malcolm who thought of it—I don't go to the garage very often.'

'Well, never mind who thought of it,' Emma pressed on gaily, aware all the time of Trent Marston's dark eyes fixed on her with cynical scrutiny, 'it was a very bright idea. The old Mini was looking decidedly the worse for wear.'

There was an awkward little silence. Emma swal-lowed. 'Oh well, then, I'll accept your offer, Mr Marston. At half-past seven?'

There was a touch of irony in the way he bowed and the dark eyes held an umistakable gleam of malice. 'Delighted,' he said.

Emma fled along the passage and up to her bed-room.

Once there she sat on the bed, breathing quickly. Trent Marston got under her skin as no man had ever done before. Although he was downstairs, talking to Uncle Edward, she could still feel his presence as if he was right here in the room. She could well understand how it had been with Lisa. Poor romantic little Lisa wouldn't have had a chance with a man like that, she would have gone down like——

She sat bolt upright suddenly. Like what? What *had* happened between them? Up to this moment she had taken it for granted that what Lisa had felt for the man had been nothing more than a romantic teenage crush. But had it? Had it been something altogether more serious? Had he seduced her? If so, that would explain a lot—Lisa's passionate outburst in the passage, her nervous fainting fit over supper last night.

She shrank from the thought. With other girls of eighteen, perhaps, it would not be so traumatic to have an affair with a man over thirty. Many of them were experienced already, as they made quite clear. But Lisa—so fastidious and delicate, such a child—no, it didn't bear thinking about. She mustn't let herself think about it. As the odious man himself had said, it was none of her business, now that Lisa was married. She would put it behind her and forget that the idea had ever occurred to her.

She got up and slid open the door of her wardrobe, debating what to wear for the party. It would be quite acceptable to keep the green bridesmaid's dress on, of course; most of the other girls would probably still be wearing their wedding gear. But she fancied something different, something that wouldn't pair her off with young Lorna, something that had been chosen by herself and not by Mrs Southall.

In the end she chose a velvet jump-suit in a beech-leaf brown that went well with her hair and her eyes and was partyish without being wispy and girlish, like the green chiffon. She took longer than usual over her make-up and chose an eyeshadow that gave a deep, almost coppery glow to her eyes, and a lipstick that provided a rich, smooth gloss. She was pleased with the final result. An up-and-coming young business woman, that was Emma Fairley. Independent. Poised. Her own girl. That horrible man would never call her an hysterical female again, not if she could help it!

He was waiting in the hall when she went downstairs at exactly half-past seven, lounging in the corner of a velvet settle, leafing through a sailing magazine. He had changed too, he looked even more spectacular in casual clothes—black cords that moulded his long legs, a dusty pink shirt and an elegant black wrapover jacket. He certainly knew how to make an impression, she thought, deciding that she'd prefer a pipe-and-tweeds man herself—if such an animal still existed.

He got up as she came down the stairs, glancing at his watch. 'On the dot,' he said. 'Are you always so punctual, Miss Fairley?'

She looked at him coldly. 'I don't claim the feminine privilege of keeping a man waiting, if that's what you mean.'

He held the front door open and she swept out before him. The low-slung silver-grey Bentley was standing in the drive. As he eased himself into the front seat beside her he said, 'That wasn't exactly what I meant. If you're going to work for me I'd like to know what to expect in the way of time-keeping.'

Fury began to stir inside her, like a smouldering volcano. 'Work for you? I wasn't aware that I was going to work *for* anybody.'

He started the car and drove slowly down the drive and along the narrow lane outside. At the turning into the main road he braked and glanced briefly at her. 'I understood from Edward that you wanted to give yourself time to learn the marketing side of the business. If so, you will certainly be working for me.' He swung the car round effortlessly. 'Perhaps your uncle hasn't had time yet to tell you about the new set-up of the firm?'

'Only that it seems you're the fairy godfather who is going to save Fairley Brothers from ruin,' she said nastily.

'And that doesn't please you?'

'No,' said Emma.

'Do you want your family firm to sink without trace, then?'

'Of course I don't,' she said crossly. 'It's the fairy godfather bit that doesn't turn me on.'

They drove in silence along the dark, hilly road. In the summer this road between the little holiday town, and the village with its Norman church and its sandy beach and sailing harbour, would be alive with traffic, but in April it was deserted. Suddenly Trent Marston asked, 'How far is this house we're making for?'

'We're nearly there,' Emma told him. 'We'll be coming into the town in two or three minutes and then the Southall house is up on the cliffs beyond.'

Abruptly he pulled the car on to the grass verge and switched off the engine and the headlights.

'It seems that there are one or two things we need to get straight while there's an opportunity,' he said. 'First, for the record, I've accepted the job of straightening things out for your firm. Your uncle has given me a free hand to do whatever is needed to get the firm on its feet again, and I believe I can do it.'

'You mean it's a takeover?'

'No.' He moved his shoulders impatiently. 'Of course it's not a takeover. Edward Fairley is the king-pin of Fairley Brothers, I'd have thought you'd know that. Without his expertise there wouldn't be a firm at all. In my opinion he's a near-genius with electronics and he's brimming over with new ideas. We plan to expand from the purely nautical navigation aids the firm is making now, into a much wider market. There's still plenty of scope for new designs in many different fields. It's the marketing side of the firm that's weak, and that's where I come in. I've got all the right contacts,' he added.

I bet you have, thought Emma. Smug, arrogant brute! But in spite of herself she felt a twinge of excitement. How lovely if Uncle Edwards's work could be given its full value and if the firm could flourish once again as it must have done when her father was alive. If only it hadn't been Trent Marston who was prepared to work the miracle. If only it had been a man she could have trusted and admired.

'And what about Joe?' she said. 'Joe Kent—our marketing manager. Does he get made redundant? Do you just step in and push out a man who has given most of his life to the firm?'

He shrugged. 'Without much success, it would seem.'

'That was exactly the reply I would have expected from you, Mr Marston,' she said icily. 'Now, may we move on, please?'

He didn't stir. 'Not just yet. There's one other thing we need to discuss.'

'I can't think of anything I want to discuss,' she said distantly. She looked out of the side window at the gorse bushes, their prickles standing out whitely in the sidelights of the car. That was how she felt sitting beside this man—prickly all over.

'We have to discuss our relationship if you're going to work for—correction, if we're going to work together.'

'Our re——' she nearly choked. 'We don't have any relationship, Mr Marston, and I'm not going to work with you!'

'Your uncle thinks otherwise,' he said smoothly, sitting back in his corner. 'He's been telling me about all the work you have put in so that you can take your place in the firm, probably rise to a directorship in a year or two. He seems to think quite highly of your capabilities.'

'That arrangement was thought of before you joined the firm, Mr Marston,' Emma said stiffly. 'Things have altered. I accept the fact that you will be much more valuable to the firm than I could possibly be—therefore I step down. To be frank, I don't like you and I couldn't work with you. I needn't explain why, I'm sure you know.'

'Because of your cousin Lisa, you mean? Are you her nanny?' he sneered. 'Did she come snivelling to you with some pathetic story of my misdeeds?'

Emma kept her temper with a huge effort, her fingernails digging into her palms. 'As a matter of fact Lisa hardly mentioned you,' she lied. 'I disliked your attitude from the first moment I saw you. But it wasn't

until I accidentally witnessed your disgusting performance outside Uncle Edward's study this afternoon
that I knew my first impression had been right.' That
was quite a sentence to get out. She was beginning to
feel utterly exhausted by this confrontation.

'All right,' he said. 'Point made—you don't like me.
I can't say that that exactly fills me with grief. But it
doesn't seem a valid reason to disappoint Edward and
change all the plans he has for you—and for the firm.
There are plenty of business relationships where love is
not lost. Sometimes it provides a cutting edge to the
proceedings. I guess I like a challenge.'

She said stubbornly, 'I shan't change my
mind.'

'You'd disappoint your uncle and upset his plans for
the sake of a silly little girl who can't bear to be out of
the limelight?'

'Oh!' she gasped. 'That's just the end, that you can
say that after the way you behaved to Lisa!' Suddenly
she wanted to hurt him as he had hurt Lisa. 'I don't
like you and I won't work with you. Is that clear, or
are you as stupid as you're callous and conceited and
insufferable?'

She felt him stiffen and heard his quick intake of
breath. He sat up as if she had pointed a gun at him
and she winced as he took her shoulders in a grasp of
steel and wrenched her round to face him.

'You little bitch,' he ground out between his teeth.
'Don't you dare speak to me like that or——' His face
was so close to hers that she could feel his breath on
her cheek. In the near-darkness she could see the dangerous glitter in his eyes.

'Or what?' she gasped, struggling to free herself. 'Do
you include violence to a woman among your other
charming habits?'

Abruptly he let her go, pushing her away from him,
and sank back into his own seat. After a moment or
two he said, 'All right, I'm sorry. But just don't go too

far, that's all.'

'That's a warning, is it?' she mocked.

'That's a warning,' he said grimly, his hand going out to the self-starter.

As the powerful car leapt forward towards the town Emma felt trickles of fear up and down her spine. Just then she had been helpless in the grip of the most powerful emotion she had ever felt in her whole life. She had *wanted* to provoke him to anger, *wanted* to lash out against him. And it wasn't only because of the way he had treated Lisa. Love and loyalty had nothing to do with it, she had to admit. It was the man himself who released some frighteningly primitive urge in her.

She would have to watch it. She would have to watch it very carefully indeed.

They drove in silence for the rest of the way, except when Emma provided Trent with directions. Through the quiet little holiday town with its Playland still boarded up, its pier closed. Up the long, steep hill to the cliff-top where rich retired people had built their white, architect-designed homes looking over the sea. Richard had already started getting out plans for a new house for himself and Lisa. Meanwhile, Lisa had told her, they would live with 'Mother.' Emma didn't envy her. Mrs Southall was amiable enough, but accustomed to ruling over her own little empire—her store, her children. But perhaps, Emma thought, Lisa wouldn't mind. She had always been so sweet and compliant. And Mrs Southall was obviously delighted with her new daughter-in-law.

The party was already in full swing when they arrived, the opulent modern house spilling light from every window on to the lawns and flowerbeds. It was cleverly built into the slope of the ground on the cliff-top and a semi-basement with wide windows provided a long playroom, the whole width of the house. From here came the dull thud of a rockbeat, much amplified.

'Oh, lord, is it that kind of party?' groaned Trent as

they got out of the car.

'Don't you dance?' Emma enquired. If he didn't then she would know exactly how to keep out of his way.

'Fortunately I escaped discomania,' he said dryly as they climbed the shallow steps to the wide front door with its ornate brass trimmings and white plaster portico.

Mrs Southall greeted them in the hall, looking elegant in a low-cut black dress, her fading fair hair pink-rinsed and immaculately coiffured, the orchid she had worn at the wedding pinned at her shoulder.

She smiled fleetingly at Emma and murmured, 'You know everyone, don't you, Emma?' and then turned a brilliant smile upon Trent. 'So glad you could come along, Mr Marston', she cooed, linking an arm with his and turning him towards the drawing room where bridge tables could be seen laid out. 'I'm sure you won't want to rampage around with the children. Too dreadfully noisy! Now, I've got so many people wanting to meet you——'

She led him away, talking gaily, smiling up into his eyes. Good heavens, thought Emma, suppressing a giggle, she's the merry widow, making a bid for the handsome, eligible bachelor. She wouldn't be more than ten or eleven years older than Trent Marston; she had been much younger than her husband who had died last year.

Good luck to her, she's welcome to him, thought Emma, and escaped down the stairs to the playroom, turning for one last look at Trent's back as he walked beside Mrs Southall, his dark head bent towards her courteously. Oh yes, he would make quite a stir among the young and the not-so-young matrons in the bridge room, with his arrogant masculine charisma. Everything about him—the taut elegance of his body, the lazy grace of his movements, the challenge of those dark eyes—would set pulses leaping; send all the respectable ladies wild with improper yearnings.

I might have been taken in myself, thought Emma. I might have gone down for the count, like poor little Lisa, if he'd turned his charms on me before I knew the kind of man he really is. What a lucky escape! She was smiling to herself as she went down the last steps into the warm, cavernous darkness of the playroom.

The atmosphere came up to meet her—the heat and the noise and the shuffle of feet on the wooden floor and the jungle beat issuing from the hi-fi equipment, mercilessly amplified. Oh yes, she could get away from Trent Marston here, it would be easy to hide in the gloom, broken only by the disco lights revolving slowly, changing from red to green, to blue to yellow, shifting over the couples twisting and turning, or locked together and moving sensuously, as the mood took them.

'Here's my girl.' Jim Bolton's voice, slightly slurred, sounded in her ear. 'I've been watching for you, my lovely. Come and have a drink.'

An arm close round her waist, he led her through the maze of dancing couples to the far end of the long room, where a table was laid and cans of beer and bottles of soft drinks and Coke and a huge bowl of punch with slices of fruit and cherries and grapes floating on the top.

Jim scooped out a long glassful for each of them. 'Good show, isn't it? Ken and George rigged up the lights themselves.' He pulled her down beside him on to cushions on the floor, and Emma realised suddenly that she was feeling very tired. But when Jim put an arm round her and drew her towards him she pulled away a little.

'Ah, c'm on, sweetheart,' he urged. 'Weddings put ideas into a fellow's head.' He buried his mouth in her neck, where the velvet jump-suit was scooped low.

Emma scrambled to her feet. 'Too early in the evening,' she said, realising with a sinking heart that Jim had already been drinking freely. 'Come and dance.'

She merged with the couples on the floor, and Jim, protesting, joined her. After a while she managed to lose him. As Mrs Southall had said, she knew everybody there. She was a year or two older than most of them. Lorna and the twins had gathered together their own circle of friends, whether they had been at the wedding or not. But in her velvet jump-suit, cut low and sleeveless, she looked younger than twenty. Ken, cutting in on one of his friends, grinned cheekily at her. 'Sexy, that's what you are, Emma.' His bright blue eyes moved appreciatively over her in the shifting lights. He had none of his brother Richard's seriousness; Ken was a whizz-kid.

They were all kids, Emma thought, an hour later, beginning to feel a headache coming on. She was tired and she wanted quite desperately to go home. She was dancing with Jim—or rather, they were shuffling round together, and his arms were round her waist, his cheek sagging against hers. She considered trying to sober him up, to ask him to drive her home, but it didn't seem a very good idea. The rest of them had paired off by now. She wondered if she could find a telephone and ring for a taxi, but if she ventured up into the main part of the house she would surely encounter some of Mrs Southall's guests, and that meant seeing Trent Marston again, which was the very last thing she wanted.

Jim was leaning heavily against her now. She pushed him away a little and put one hand to her throbbing head and thought longingly of slipping into a cool bed and closing her eyes.

'Mine, I think,' murmured a deep voice close above her. In one swift movement she was detached from Jim, who seemed to dissolve into the gloom, and she found herself in Trent's arms, and moving to the music.

The sheer physical shock of feeling his hard, taut

body against hers after Jim Bolton's slackness left her speechless, her heart thumping. Then she pulled herself together. 'I—I thought you didn't dance,' she said idiotically.

'Did you now?' His voice was deep and soft, just above her ear, giving the words an intimacy that sent an odd shiver through her. 'Perhaps there are one or two other things about me that you got wrong.'

Emma was utterly confused. This was the man she hated, that she had been desperate to keep away from, and yet the sensations that were coursing through her as his body pressed against hers were overwhelming.

'Let's dance,' he went on huskily, his hands moving up and down her back on the softness of the velvet. 'You feel like a kitten, a beautiful strokeable kitten.'

She groped desperately for sanity. 'I have claws,' she said.

He rubbed his cheek against her hair. 'Oh, I know all about that. They scratch but don't go very deep. Now, don't talk, just enjoy the dance.'

He was a wonderful dancer, of course. She had never had a partner like him. They moved together to the languor of the beat, in perfect unison as if their two bodies were one. I must be mad, she thought wildly. I've drunk too much of that punch, it must be more potent than I thought. She ought to pull away from him, but his arm around her was like sprung steel holding her close, thigh to thigh, the soft swelling of her breast against his muscled hardness. She'd been so right about him—he was danger, he was temptation. She *had* to fight it, she had to.

Summoning every bit of will-power, she pulled away fom him, stopped dancing. He still held her, loosely now. 'What's the matter?' he asked, looking down into her face.

'I—I——' Her voice refused to function. She stared up into the strong, hard face above her own and as she did so a crimson glow passed over it from the disco lights. He looks like the devil, she thought faintly.

But his voice was unexpectedly gentle as he said,
'You're tired, aren't you? You've had a hectic two days,
you need a good night's sleep. Come along, I'll take
you home. That's why I came to find you. I've had
enough of the skittish ladies in the bridge room.'

Heaven, she thought, to get home and slide into a
cool bed. But to travel back in the car beside Trent?
She'd planned to ask Jim to see her home, and now,
after the way she had just been feeling, that seemed
even more advisable.

'But—but we can't leave so early——' she faltered.

He led her to the side of the room. 'You just watch
us.'

'And—and I half promised to go home with Jim
Bolton,' she said weakly. 'You know—the best man and
the chief bridesmaid, it's a sort of ritual that they pair
off for the rest of the day.'

She looked round for Jim and spotted him slumped
on the floor near one of the hi-fi loudspeakers. He
didn't seem conscious of the booming sound issuing
from it. In fact, he didn't seem conscious of anything.

Trent followed her glance. 'He won't miss you,' he
said dryly. 'Come along.'

At the top of the stairs they encountered Mrs
Southall. 'Emma's feeling all in,' Trent told her. 'I
know you'll understand if I take her off home now. All
the excitement of the wedding and no doubt a spot of
jet-lag too.'

Mrs Southall's light blue eyes passed over her. 'Poor
Emma,' she said coolly. 'Of course you must go home
straight away. But there's no need for you to rush away
so soon, Trent.' She said his name coyly. 'My chauffeur will see Emma home safely.'

'Many thanks, but I'll drive her myself.' His smile
and his tone were pleasant enough, but somehow he
conveyed that any further argument would be quite
useless. 'Have you a wrap, Emma?'

Five minutes later, after thanks and further apologies, she found herself sitting beside Trent, driving back the way they had come.

Now what? she thought nervously, watching the way his hand rested on the wheel, lightly and yet with complete control. Had he just been making an excuse to get her to himself in the seclusion of his car, to continue what he had certainly started on the dance floor? A tremor ran through her from head to foot.

They drove through the sleepy little town and up the hill on the other side into the blackness of the country road again, the headlights cleaving a dazzling white path ahead. Trent didn't say a single word until he stopped the car outside the front door of the old grey house, all in darkness except for the light from the hall window. Then he switched off the engine and turned towards her and smiled. 'Delivered safe and sound,' he said.

'Thank you,' said Emma. That smile was almost more disturbing than the touch of his hands had been.

They sat looking at each other in the dim silence inside the car. Emma felt her heart thumping against the velvet of her jump-suit.

Then, slowly, his arm came up and slid along the back of the seat and he leaned towards her. After a moment, when she could have drawn away if she had had the power to do so, his hand dropped to her shoulder, closed round her neck and he drew her slowly towards him.

Sanity left her completely and she was engulfed in an almost feverish hunger for his kiss. When his mouth closed over hers she let out a small moan and her arms went up to clasp themselves behind his dark head and draw him even nearer, while her lips and mouth responded to his with a wildness that seemed to have nothing to do with the girl she had thought she was until now.

She felt the pounding of his own heart and knew he

was aroused too. For a moment his arms tightened round her, then with a little shake of his head he let her go, pushing her away gently.

'Thank you, Emma, that was nice,' he said. 'Who was it remarked that weddings are for kissing? Your friend the best man, wasn't it? Now you must get along to bed and get some sleep. I've got some things to talk over with your uncle. I see he's still working.' He jerked his head towards where lights showed in the workroom at the end of the garden. 'I'll tell him we're hitting it off very well, shall I?'

Emma had heard about blinding flashes of insight, when everything becomes clear in a second. She had one now. Of course—Trent Marston had been practising his charms on her for one reason only. He was so sure of himself that he knew she would fall for him and wouldn't be likely to say anything to Uncle Edward about the affair between Lisa and himself.

Uncle Edward, tucked away in his workroom, wouldn't have seen what was going on under his own eyes. But if he found out that Trent had hurt his beloved daughter that would alter everything. Edward Fairley was a mild man, but he would undoubtedly show Trent the door, and the firm would then proceed downhill even more rapidly.

Emma got out of the car. She was ice-cold now. As Trent slammed the door on his side and walked round to her she said calmly, 'You're keen on taking this work on for the firm, aren't you?'

She saw his eyebrows go up. 'Yes, I am. Why ask now?'

'I merely wanted to assure you that I've no intention of doing anything to stand in your way. Or of doing anything to help you either. Thank you for the lift home, Mr Marston,' she added, and turning abruptly she walked into the house and left him standing there staring after her.

CHAPTER FOUR

THE house was silent. In the hall every trace of the reception had been tidied away and the wedding might never have been. Jessie and Malcolm must have been working at it all evening and they must have already gone to bed, tired out.

Emma went out to the kitchen, switched on the light and filled the kettle. A cup of tea might restore a semblance of normality to the evening. She sat down to drink it at the big old-fashioned wooden table that Jessie refused to part with and scrubbed lovingly every day.

After the first cup of tea, sanity began to return, but she still felt more churned up inside than she had ever felt before. What had possessed her to behave as she had just done, out there in the car? Tiredness? Jet-lag? Too many glasses of punch?

No, face it, Emma, the man was devastating. He had gone through her defences like a laser beam went through—whatever laser beams *did* go through. From the first moment she set eyes on him he had given her one look and all her inside workings had begun to quiver like a jelly, she thought with bitter self-contempt. And what had just happened had been the final humiliating result.

She pulled her thoughts up short. But what actually *had* happened? She had danced with a man. He had driven her home. He had kissed her in the car. Nothing world-shattering about that—it had happened before.

Ah, but never like that! Never that wild, heady ecstasy that had made her cling to him, snuggle into his arms like the kitten he had called her. For a few moments she had been overwhelmed by a kind of madness, but not again. No, she had to admit the sheer animal magnetism of the man, and then proceed to take herself out of its field of attraction.

She knew the danger. She knew the way he treated women. She winced, hearing again the cruel bite of his voice saying, 'I don't love you, never did. I don't give a damn for you, Lisa.'

That was the kind of man he was, a man who would amuse himself with a girl and then throw her aside with callous brutality. She didn't intend to be his next victim. She would see Uncle Edward tomorrow and tell him she would prefer to spend another year on her languages—in Greece, or Germany, perhaps—before she took her place in a senior position in the firm. It shouldn't be too difficult to convince him without telling him the true reason—that Trent Marston had come close to breaking his young daughter's heart. Trent Marston seemed to be the firm's last hope. Therefore he must stay and she must go.

Not merely because she hated him and feared him, she admitted, as she dragged herself upstairs to bed. But because she was afraid of herself.

It was quite a time before she went to sleep. She kept on waking up and thinking about what had happened and what a fool she was to let herself get carried away by a man who specialised in trading on his sex-appeal. And when she did go to sleep she dreamed that she was standing naked on the bank of a fast-flowing river. Trent Marston was swimming towards her with powerful strokes, brown arms flailing the turbulent water, and calling, 'Come on, Emma darling, jump in, I'll catch you.'

She didn't need Freud to tell her what that meant. She took it as another warning.

When she finally sank into sleep she slept heavily and wakened to see Jessie standing beside the bed with a tray in her hands.

Emma shot up, pushing the hair away from her

flushed face. 'Heavens, what time is it? Jessie, you shouldn't have brought my breakfast up—I'm just a lazy so-and-so.'

Jessie plonked the tray down and drew the curtains back. 'Och, no, Miss Emma, you earned a good lie-in. Flying all those thousands of miles across the sea and then all the excitement of the wedding and you having to look after Miss Lisa, and very prettily you did it too. You needed a guid long night.'

'And so did you, Jessie. You must have worked like a beaver, clearing everything up after I went out to Mrs Southall's party.'

Jessie's face creased into the nearest thing to a smile she ever allowed herself. 'You enjoyed it? I saw you go off with Mr Marston.'

Emma bent her head over the coffee pot. 'Jessie, why all the dark hints about me and Mr Marston? I assure you I don't like the man at all.'

Jessie picked up the top of a jar of cleansing cream that Emma had left lying on the dressing-table last night, and screwed it on again firmly. Her smile became even more enigmatic. 'Oh, aye?' she said on her way to the door. 'I didna think much of Malcolm when I met him, either.'

She went out on to the landing, then her head appeared round the door again. 'Mr Edward's down in the workroom. He said to ask you to go and see him, but there was no hurry. Mr Marston went off early to the factory, so you tak' your time and enjoy your breakfast.'

Emma found she was hungry. She had drunk several glasses of punch last night and eaten nothing except a couple of biscuits with her cup of tea when she got home. Now she cracked the top off a brown egg and spread creamy Dorset butter on her toast and proceeded to enjoy herself. She was getting over last night, it couldn't have made all that much impression on her after all. What's in a kiss? she asked herself, crunching toast pleasurably.

She browsed over the subject as she ate her breakfast. She was nearly twenty-one, and she would have had to have been very stupid not to know that men found her attractive. There had been plenty of kisses in her life, and the funny thing was that every kiss was different from every other. It must be like fingerprints, she thought with a grin. No man kissed you in exactly the same way as any other man.

She drank up her coffee and went along to the bathroom for her shower. What was she thinking of—maundering on to herself about kisses at this time in the morning? A cool shower would put all that nonsense out of her head.

The odd thing was that it didn't. As she soaped her smooth body under the tepid water and dried the pinkly glowing limbs with a fleecy towel, she was still thinking about kisses—and one particular kiss at that.

As soon as she got downstairs the phone rang and it was Jim Bolton. 'Emma? What happened to you last night? You disappeared. Are you okay? Mrs Southall said you'd gone home early, you had a headache. Why didn't you say? I'd have driven you home.' He sounded half-way between huffiness and guilt.

'I was going to ask you, but you were drunk,' Emma said bluntly.

'I was *not* drunk!' he spluttered loudly. There was a sudden pause and she could see him looking round the estate agent's office where he worked to see if anyone was listening. In a lowered tone he said, 'Okay, Emma, perhaps I was a mite over the limit and I'm sorry if I let you down. We'd all had rather too much—old Richard was in a flat spin before the wedding and I had to bolster him up a bit, and then afterwards—oh well, I'm sorry if I was a clot, love. It won't happen again. Forgive me?'

She laughed. 'Of course,' she said. 'Weddings are

for celebrating, aren't they?' And for kissing, she thought, with a jolt of her stomach as she heard again a deep, amused voice, felt the touch of strong fingers at the nape of her neck, smelled the clean fragrance of a man's freshly-washed hair against her cheek.

She dragged her mind back to what Jim was saying. '—lunch, can you manage it? Just to show I'm forgiven.'

'Lunch?' she echoed vaguely. 'Today?'

'Yes, today. I can get away at twelve, with any luck. I've got to take a potential customer to look over a bungalow in Worth Matravers, but after that I'm free. We'll meet at the Golden Butterfly as usual, shall we?'

Emma didn't really want to lunch with Jim, there were too many other things on her mind, but at least she would be away from the house, and any risk of encountering Trent Marston. Jim worked in Poole, and the factory and office of Fairley Brothers were in that town too. But Trent wasn't likely to lunch at the Golden Butterfly. The three-star Dolphin in the High Street would be more his style. So she agreed to meet Jim and he sounded delighted, and she had a feeling that he was going to ask her again to marry him.

She sighed as she made her way down the garden to Uncle Edward's workroom. She had told Jim 'No' so many times, but he wouldn't take it, and if there was anything she hated, it was having pressure put on, and made to feel she was letting someone down.

Uncle Edward looked up as she knocked and went into the workroom. He smiled at her and she smiled back and thought, with a sudden surge of affection, that he really was the nicest of men. His gold-rimmed glasses were perched on the end of his nose, giving him a decided look of the 'mad professor' that she and Jessie had jokingly named him. He was not yet fifty, she knew, but he looked older. Tragedy and worry and his somewhat one-pointed existence had put grey in his hair and wrinkles on his face.

'Busy?' Emma enquired, which wasn't necessary, for he was always busy.

He held up two crossed fingers, and his blue eyes shone keenly behind his glasses. 'I think I may be on to something that will make all our fortunes.'

'Great!'

'Marston thinks so too.' He nodded thoughtfully. 'You know, Emma, for a man who doesn't profess to be a boffin, that chap has a superb grasp of technology. A very bright brain indeed.'

'Yes,' said Emma, 'I'd rather gathered that.' He'd thought out his plan last night very cleverly.

Edward put down his pencil and swivelled round in his chair. 'I'm glad you're getting on with him. He seems very impressed with you. I think you'll make a very good team. When this new thing really gets cracking we're going to need all the expertise we can get.'

She drew a finger along the edge of the work-bench. 'I wanted to talk to you about that, Uncle Edward. Meeting a man like Trent has shown me that I don't have what it takes to work with him yet. As you say, he's a live wire; he'll expect more than I can give.' (And you can say that again, Emma!) 'I thought,' she went on carefully, 'that if I could have another year, perhaps, to work on my languages? I could go back to Germany and stay with Hallbachs, they'll take me any time, they said so. Then, perhaps, six months in Greece? My Spanish and French are fairly good and I can get by in Italian. But I'd like to be really confident before I take up the job. Dear old Joe isn't critical, but Mr Marston would be, I'm sure. What do you say?'

He looked disappointed. 'Are you sure, Emma? We were planning on Trent making up his marketing team straight away, and he seems keen to include you.'

Yes, she thought, and I know why—because he wants to keep things sweet between us in case I decide to tell Uncle Edward what a bastard he is in his private life. Probably the very qualities of hardness and ruthlessness that she knew he possessed would make him a success in business. Emma didn't know and she didn't propose to find out. She knew enough of her uncle to guess that he would feel the same way.

Perhaps she ought to tell him—perhaps it wasn't fair to keep him in the dark about the character of the man he seemed to be putting all his trust in. But that would mean the break-up of the firm, for sure. She couldn't take the responsibility for that.

She said, 'He's only keen to include me because I happen to be your niece. He can't have any idea of my capabilities yet, I only met him yesterday and we haven't talked business at all.'

A little sheepishly Edward Fairley said, 'I showed him a letter I had from Joe, saying quite a lot about your capabilities. Joe was most impressed with the report you compiled for him.'

'Yes,' she said, quckly changing the subject, 'and that's another thing. What about Joe? How is this new appointment going to affect him? He's so devoted to the firm and he's worked like a brick all the time we've been in the U.S. It seems——' she paused. She needed to be tactful about this— 'don't you think it seems a bit hard to bring in an outsider above him? I suppose that's what it would amount to.'

It was a moment before he replied, then he said with unusual seriousness, 'I know you think the world of Joe, Emma. So do I, and I wouldn't do anything that would hurt or distress him. But we had a long talk before you and he left on this trip and he confessed to me that he hoped it would be the last overseas commitment he was asked to undertake. He was very reluctant to upset the pattern, but he said he'd felt for some time now that he wasn't doing justice to the job. It was all getting a bit too much for him and he wished we could find someone to take on most of the promotional work and allow him to spend his time more on the routine, based in the office. I've no doubt at all that he'll be delighted when he hears about the change, and when he gets back from Mexico next week we can all put our heads together and work something out.'

He sighed and passed a hand rather wearily across his brow. 'If you only knew, Emma, how much it will mean to me to have a younger, more dynamic man in charge of that part of the business I can't handle.' He looked out through the window. 'Your father was the man—you know that—and together we could have tackled anything. I've waited a long time to find someone else.'

Emma said, holding all emotion out of her voice, 'You don't feel bad about putting another man in Father's place?'

'Not if it's Trent Marston,' he said simply. 'I just feel he's the right one.'

She bit her lip. 'Then you think I shouldn't go to Germany?'

'Oh, don't let's be hasty about it. We'll all meet and discuss it this evening. Meanwhile——' he picked up a folder— 'I wonder if you'd go along to the office with this, Emma? I promised Trent you'd take it to him there as soon as I'd finished it. He went out early this morning. Malcolm's working in the garden, so you can take the Rover. Will you do that for me?'

Her first impulse was to find some excuse, so that she wouldn't have to confront Trent Marston this morning, but she overcame the impulse rapidly. It would be childish to behave like that, and why should he have the power to affect her actions? She raised her head. 'Of course I'll go,' she said briskly. 'I'll go straight away. I was going into Poole this morning in any case—I promised to have lunch with Jim.'

Edward nodded absently. 'Oh yes? Well, enjoy yourself.' Already his attention was back on his work.

Emma went out and left him to it. The interview

had certainly not been an unqualified success. But Uncle Edward hadn't definitely said 'No,' to her idea. She would work on it again this evening. Somehow she had to get herself out of Trent Marston's field of activity.

Half an hour later Emma was parking the Rover outside the Fairley Brothers premises in Poole. The factory, of which the office was a part, was in the old district of Poole, near the quay. It had originally been a boatbuilding yard, which also made and supplied other items of sailing equipment. After the war, when her grandfather died, it had gradually narrowed down to specialising in navigational instruments, which were Uncle Edward's particular field of interest. Half of the building had been sold off and was now used as a café, which was open only during the summer season.

Emma was always aware, these days, of a faint depression when she visited the factory. Now she parked the car and sat for a moment or two, looking at the outside, at the big doors that had once opened on to a thriving boatyard; at the seedy café next door, its windows boarded up against vandalism, the door covered with peeling posters.

How splendid if the whole place could be smartened up and put on its feet again! Much as she hated the idea of Trent Marston coming here and taking over, it seemed that he was their last hope.

She took the folder from the front seat and locked up the car, glancing at her watch. It was a quarter to twelve. Just time to hand over the folder and walk to the Golden Butterfly to meet Jim. That would save having to hunt for somewhere to park the car in the centre of town.

As she slid open the heavy door her inside stirred uneasily at the prospect of seeing Trent Marston again, after last night. She would be very brief, very businesslike, just hand him the folder and leave.

Inside the big room, the six trained girls, whose job

it was to assemble the intricate parts of the navigation instruments, bent over their work-tables. Emma paused for a moment or two for a word with a couple of the ones she knew best. They were a good, loyal work-force; Uncle Edward paid them well and they adored him—and Joe too. It was like a big happy family.

Ted Draper, the foreman, hailed Emma from across the floor. 'Hullo, Miss Emma, home again? Had a good time?' He was a hefty, tow-headed man who had a tiny, neat wife. They had produced three children, and Emma paused to ask after them.

'I've come with a folder to leave in the office,' she said. 'Is there somebody there?'

'The new boss,' said Ted, deadpan.

She studied his face and learned nothing from it. 'How's he getting along? What do you think?'

'I'll wait a bit and see,' said Ted, ever-cautious. He jerked his big head towards the girls at the work-tables. 'He's caused quite a flutter among that lot,' he said dryly.

Yes, Emma thought, he would. He'd only have to flash that dark, smouldering glance of his around to have them all working at double speed. Her dislike of the man and his tactics moved up another notch.

They talked for a moment longer about Joe. Emma said she thought he seemed rather tired when she left him and Ted nodded as if he knew all about that. Then she smiled goodbye and went through the glass door into the office.

'Good morning, Miss Fairley,' chirped the new little typist brightly. And 'Good morning, Miss Fairley, nice to see you again, have you enjoyed the tour?' offered Rose, Joe's middle-aged secretary. She'd had a colour-rinse and a new curly hair-style. She wore a frilly white blouse and a rather too-tight skirt. Her cheeks were pink and her eyes were shining. 'Mr Marston's in the private office,' she said, with what amounted to a simper.

Oh lord, you too! thought Emma in disgust, and marched into the smaller room at the far end of the office.

Trent was sitting at the big desk, surrounded by files and ledgers. He looked up when the door opened and a slow smile touched his mouth at the corners. 'Well, well, I am honoured. I was expecting Malcolm to be the courier.'

She had been prepared to feel a trifle embarrassed when they met again after that prolonged kiss in his car last night. What she hadn't been expecting was the flood of awareness that sent a tingle all through her body as she met those dark, lazy eyes with their absurdly long, curving lashes.

She put the folder on the desk. 'Uncle Edward asked me to bring this,' she said, and turned to the door again.

'Wait a bit,' Trent said quietly. 'Why the hurry?'

'I've got an appointment for lunch at twelve o'clock,' she gabbled, one hand on the door handle. 'I've only just got time to walk into town.'

He was on his feet now, standing beside her. 'My car's here, I'll run you there,' he said. 'Now, come and sit down.'

The next moment she found herself sitting opposite him across the desk. 'What do you want?' she asked in a strangled kind of voice. The way he was looking at her was sending shock waves up and down her spine.

'Just to look at you,' he said, and proceeded to do so.

She sat staring back at him, gradually feeling a sort of creeping paralysis taking over; to have someone look at you in silence, she thought helplessly, was the most agonising thing there was. She swallowed, which was an effort with a completely dry throat, and said, 'I hope you aren't thinking of buying. The goods aren't for sale.'

He laughed then. It was the first time she had heard him laugh, deep and low and velvety, like a caress, and that shook her too. Heavens, the man was dynamite!

'Relax,' he said. 'I'm not—for the moment—bidding in the sort of market you have in mind; I was merely assessing your possible usefulness in other ways. Ways that would be of benefit to the firm, of course.'

'Really?' she said with heavy sarcasm.

'Yes, really. I like your style very much, including your taste in clothes. That colour—burnt orange, would you call it?—goes particularly well with your hair and your eyes. It brings a note of cheer to a dull day.'

'Thank you very much,' said Emma. 'Is that all you have to say to me, because——'

'I can just see you,' he mused on, as if she hadn't spoken, 'drawing the crowd at a big trade exhibition, attracting potential customers to the Fairley Brothers stand. There's nothing like a pretty girl to boost business. Look at the Motor Show.'

She felt fury boiling up inside her. She clenched her fists. '*You* may see me decorating an exhibition stand, Mr Marston,' she said hotly. 'I have quite different ideas about my usefulness to the firm. Please remember that.'

He smiled with relish and she realised with vexation that she had played straight into his hands. He was the kind of man who enjoyed a fight. 'Sheathe those claws, Emma. You'd be a decoration in any place, exhibition stand or not. Don't tell me you'd rather be a collar-and-tie-and-no-make-up type of woman executive. And I'm sure your talents extend into many other fields. Many others.' He gazed up at the ceiling and then down at that part of her body, swelling prettily behind its lightweight woollen jacket, that was visible above the desk.

'Oh!' she gasped furiously. 'You're hateful and impossible!'

'Thanks,' he said coolly. He got to his feet. 'Now, as I said, I'll give you a lift into town, if you're leaving your car here. I have to see my bank manager.'

He put a hand at her elbow as they passed through the outer office and the factory workroom. All the women were aware of him as they went by—it was like a ripple passing through the room. They were probably envying her, Emma thought bitterly, pushing her way forward round a machine, so that she could disengage herself from the light hold on her arm. His touch seemed to burn through the sleeve of her jacket.

'Where can I drop you?' asked Trent as he nosed the Bentley out into the street from the factory yard.

'Oh, anywhere in the centre of the town will do,' she said hurriedly. The smell of the expensive leather and the soft cushiony feel of the upholstery inside the car were touching up memories of last night much too keenly, and she wanted to get out as soon as she could.

'Oh no, please allow me to deliver you to the door. I kept you, and I shouldn't like to think I'd made you late for your appointment.'

There was no getting the better of this man, was there? 'The Golden Butterfly,' she said briefly.

'Ah, yes, I know exactly where it is. A pleasant little restaurant.'

Something in his voice made her look up sharply. He knew it, then? Had he brought Lisa here? The words of the letter came back to her: 'I'm swinging on a star, sliding down a rainbow, Trent's taking me out to dinner tonight.'

And then he would drive Lisa home, poor little Lisa who hadn't a clue, then, about the kind of man he really was. And in the darkness he would take her in his arms and kiss her, as he had kissed Emma last night. A shudder passed through her and she couldn't get out of the car quickly enough. As soon as it stopped she almost fell out and slammed the door.

'Thanks for the lift,' she said, without looking at

him, and ran into the restaurant.

As she went into the small, comfortable bar where she always met Jim the clock showed five past twelve, but Jim hadn't arrived yet. She sat down in a corner to wait. After a few minutes Jacques, the head waiter, came across to her. 'Ah, Mees Fairley, Mr Bolton 'ave just telephone. 'e is sorry he will be a leetle late and ask you please to wait. May I get you a drink while you wait? Your usual?'

He brought her favourite lime and lemon, with a dash of angostura, and beamed as he left her.

Half an hour later she was still waiting. She knew lots of people in Poole and had met and chatted with two friends, consumed another drink, and was beginning to feel very hungry, and to debate whether she should go into the restaurant and start lunch on her own.

Then the door from the street opened and Trent Marston walked in. He stood looking around him with his usual arrogant air, and Emma felt a curious tug at the pit of her stomach as his eyes lighted on her.

He came over to the table. 'Boy-friend stood you up?' he smiled.

'He's been delayed,' Emma said with as much dignity as she could manage.

He looked pointedly at his watch. 'Half an hour is much too long to keep a girl hanging around waiting for her lunch.'

'I am *not* hanging around.' She tried to freeze him, but it wasn't easy when she had to look up about half a mile to see his face. 'Jim never knows exactly when he's going to get away when he's interviewing a client about buying a house. I quite understand.' She wondered why she felt she had to justify herself or apologise for Jim.

He dropped into a seat beside her. 'Well, let's order lunch, shall we? Then if Jim-boy does put in an appearance I'll remove myself.'

He didn't wait for her to agree. He held up a finger and Jacques appeared like the genie of the lamp. This was the kind of man who can make head waiters appear out of nowhere. Money talks, Emma thought sourly.

'Miss Fairley and I will get on with lunch, Jacques.'

'Vairy good, Mr Marston.' Jacques produced large menu cards.

'Steak?' Trent enquired, looking at Emma with all the courtesy of a considerate host wishing to make a good impression on his guest. 'They do an excellent steak here.'

She shook her head. If she had to eat lunch with this man she would need something that would go down more easily than a steak. 'I'll have scampi,' she said.

She kept hoping that Jim would arrive before their lunch was served, but there was no sign of him. Trent seemed quite at ease, sipping his drink and making small talk about Poole, which town he seemed to know well, and about boats and sailing. He was in the process of buying a sea-going yacht, he mentioned, as casually as if he were talking about buying a rubber dinghy. 'You must help me to christen her when she's delivered,' he said, to which Emma didn't consider it necessary to reply.

After ten minutes Jacques reappeared. 'Your lunch is ready, sir.' He smiled broadly from one to the other of them. Evidently Jacques, too, thought Emma was doing very well for herself, lunching with Trent Marston. It was too maddening for words.

She gave a final despairing glance towards the door as she stood up. Trent followed her eyes. 'Shame!' he said dryly. 'You'll have to put up with me, I'm afraid.'

They were ushered into the restaurant, which was filling up quickly, and seated at a side table. Emma drank her tomato soup with appreciation and made no attempt to play the grateful guest and sparkle with conversation. Trent had made a point of lunching with her and he must have some reason for wanting to do so. It couldn't be that her company gave him any pleasure; not after the way she had done everything she could to discourage him.

She gave up wondering, and settled down to enjoy the food. The scampi were delicious—as golden and crisp and crunchy as scampi ought to be. Trent ordered a carafe of white wine that tasted coolly of flowers. If any other man but Trent Marston had been sitting opposite it would have been a really enjoyable occasion, but it was no good pretending that she could be completely easy in his company. In spite of the good food and the wine she felt as defensive and uncomfortable as she had ever felt in her life.

For a time they ate in silence and then Trent put down his knife and fork, sipped his wine, and said, 'The bank manager was very amiable.'

So they were going to talk business, were they? That suited her.

'Good,' she said briskly. 'That's quite a change for Fairley Brothers. I suppose the company will be heavily in your debt? You can't expand in the way you're intending to without putting in a good deal of fresh capital, can you?'

He shrugged and started on his steak again. 'No problem. The reason I'm here at all is that I find myself with a good deal of spare capital to invest.'

'So what will your position be? You're buying yourself a directorship?'

'I suppose that's the way it is.'

'I see,' said Emma coolly. So much for Uncle Edward's fond hopes of making *her* a director in the future! She couldn't see herself sitting at a boardroom table discussing business with Trent Marston. She was sure they would disagree on every possible point. The present atmosphere in the firm of 'one big happy family' would surely not survive the impact of a ruthless go-getter.

She looked across the table at him—at the handsome,

hard face with its flesh drawn tight over high cheek-bones, the mouth chiselled yet sensual, the brooding, liquid-dark eyes—

She swallowed, searching for words. At last she managed lamely, 'For someone who's just come into the firm you seem very dedicated, Mr Marston.'

He sat back in his chair, the arrogant half-smile touching his lips. 'I *am* very dedicated. I never take on anything that doesn't hold out a promise of success.'

'And Fairley Brothers does? You do surprise me. I don't pretend to be an expert, but I know the state our finances are in—rocky.'

'Good. If you know, then that saves me from explaining the situation.'

She lifted her eyebrows. 'I—don't understand.'

'No, obviously you don't. In fact——' his voice was touched with mockery—'you don't understand me in the least yet, do you, Emma? Briefly, I like a challenge. I like rescue work when I come across something worth rescuing. Have you been into your uncle's workshop recently?'

'Yes, of course. Why?'

'You're aware that he's been working on some completely new technology?'

'Well, yes. He said something about a break-through.'

'And that's all you know?'

She began to lose her temper. 'What do you expect me to know? I'm not an electronics wizard.'

Very calmly he said, 'I didn't suggest you were. Fortunately, your uncle is—a wizard, I mean. I've met quite a few original minds working in his area, but his ideas completely shattered me.'

She stared at him. 'Is he really that good? I didn't realise.'

'He's a bloody marvel,' said Trent simply, and it didn't occur to her to question his opinion. Trent Marston knew what he was talking about.

'His ideas are spreading out into all sorts of possibilities,' he went on. He leaned forward across the table towards her. 'Like it or not, Emma, we're near the beginning of the electronic revolution—we don't know a hundredth part of it yet, only that it has to happen. And as it has to happen I believe we should go all out to make sure that the instruments and machines we make are worth making, the very best of their kind.' His dark eyes were glittering as if he were seeing a vision of the future.

Suddenly she knew what Uncle Edward meant when he said that this man was dynamic. She could still remember how her father's eyes had shone like this when he talked about what he meant to do with the family firm, how he was going to take it into the 'big time.' Only his eyes were blue and clear and candid and open—not the dark, vaguely menacing eyes of the man sitting opposite her.

But in spite of her personal opinion of Trent Marston, she couldn't help a small thrill of pleasure at his words. How wonderful to think of Fairley Brothers throbbing away again, competing in the market and not slowly drifting downhill for want of a business brain at the head of things. To think of the loyal staff being removed from the threat of the dole queue, and Uncle Edward's work being recognised and valued.

If Trent Marston could accomplish the miracle, then good luck to him. But he would have to do it without her. She didn't believe for one moment that he would care if she decided to opt out—just so long as she didn't try to undermine Uncle Edward's good opinion of his—Trent's—integrity. She didn't take seriously the remarks he had made back in the office about her appearance; he was merely flattering her for a purpose. He would manipulate people without thinking twice about it, if it suited him. That was what he had been doing last night in the car.

He had just said that she didn't understand him.

But she did, and she was sure she was right. He was a man dedicated to power and success above everything else and he would ruthlessly discard anything and anyone who got in his way. Similarly, he would use and manipulate anyone he thought could help him. Until—she guessed—their usefulness was at an end, when they would be thrown on the scrap-heap with the rest.

That was her opinion of him—she thought him despicable. But a certain fair-mindedness (or was it a faint hope that she might be wrong?) made her say, 'You seem to have formed a high opinion of Uncle Edward. Has he, do you think, formed an equally accurate opinion of you?'

He went very still, his eyes suddenly watchful. 'What are you implying?'

Her heart began to beat uncomfortably quickly, but she had started this and she had to go on. 'I think you know. I wonder if he would have such a good opinion of your character if he knew the details of the way you'd treated his daughter, which I'm sure he doesn't. I don't believe he has any idea of what went on between you.'

For a second she saw pure anger drain the colour from his face. Then, almost immediately, he had control of himself again.

'I think you're right,' he said very dryly. 'I'm quite sure he doesn't know.'

'And you wouldn't like him to know?'

'I would very much prefer,' he said, weighing his words carefully, 'to keep the details of that small episode from him, if possible.'

She nodded, pressing her lips together contemptuously. 'Yes, I can well understand *that*. And you thought I might tell him, didn't you? That was your reason for staging another "small episode" with me, last night in your car? It was all carefully thought out, wasn't it?'

He regarded her in silence for a time, his dark eyes brooding. Then he said, 'It wasn't the only reason. But I admit I wanted to soften that rather harsh judgment you seem to have of me, yes.'

'And you thought your overpowering masculine technique would do the trick?' she lashed at him.

A gleam came into his eyes. 'I've found it the quickest and most pleasant way to make up a quarrel.'

'Well, it didn't work with me. It didn't impress me in the least,' she said disdainfully.

'No? I thought you seemed to be enjoying it.'

'I was tired and I'd had too much to drink on an empty stomach,' she snapped.

Trent laughed aloud, the gleam in his eye pure amusement now. He leaned over and filled up her glass. 'I must remember that for future occasions.'

Emma was saved from trying to think of a retort to that because at that moment Jim came rushing in, barging between the tables, his face pink, and worry-lines engraved between his fair eyebrows. He came straight over to Emma and leaned over her chair, without a glance at Trent.

'Sweetheart, I'm so sorry about this, but I couldn't let the chance of a sale go. The bungalow out at Worth has been on the market for months and I saw a chance of hooking this bloke.' He groaned. 'He went round everywhere about twelve times and he did everything bar digging the place up to inspect the foundations. He even lifted the carpets looking for woodworm.' He ran a hand frantically through his light brown hair.

'And is he buying?' Emma enquired brightly, pointedly turning away from Trent to express interest in Jim's business deal.

'I've got him in the office now, I'll have to dash back before he changes his mind. Forgive me, darling? You've had lunch, I see—that's splendid. I'll tell Jacques to book it up to my account.'

Trent had been leaning back in his chair, listening

to this exchange with interest. Now he said quietly and incisively, 'Miss Fairley happens to be lunching with me, old man. I'm afraid you missed the boat.'

Jim goggled as he saw for the first time that Trent and Emma were together. 'Oh—I—I didn't see——'

Emma took pity on him. 'Mr Marston and I have been having a working lunch, Jim, as you'd evidently been detained. Mr Marston is our new director in the firm—did you meet him at the wedding yesterday?'

'Oh, I——' Jim gulped. 'I believe I——' He pulled himself together. 'Oh well, so long as you've had lunch. Good show, then, Em. I'll ring you. Lots of sorries, again.'

He dashed out.

Trent sipped the remains of his wine. 'Now there,' he mused, 'is a man wedded to his job. I like that.'

Emma glared at him speechlessly, longing to pick up the whole carafe and throw it in his face. But at that moment Jacques approached the table.

'Mr Fairley is on the phone, Miss Fairley. 'e ask could you come and speak to him.'

She was on her feet immediately, relieved to get away from Trent, determined to make Uncle Edward's call, whatever it was, an excuse to avoid Trent Marston's company for the rest of the day.

She picked up the receiver in the small telephone room along the passage. 'Uncle Edward?'

'Emma dear—I thought I might catch you. Listen, Emma, it's rather upsetting news, I'm afraid. I've just had a call from Mexico City, from a hospital there. Poor old Joe has been taken seriously ill. It happened last night, but they've only just found out who to contact.'

She was suddenly cold all over. 'He's not—how is he?'

'It was difficult to make out.' Uncle Edward sounded desperately worried. 'Whoever it was didn't speak very good English and you know I don't understand

Spanish. I think they said it was probably his heart, but I couldn't be sure. Oh, Emma dear, what should we do?'

'I must go out to him straight away,' she said without hesitation. 'I can, can't I, Uncle? He hasn't anyone of his own.'

'Yes, of course you can, Emma. But all that flying—and booking a passage—and—oh, dear, it's all so complicated.'

'Now, don't you worry, Uncle Edward, I'll cope. I'll get out there quickly somehow. I'll come home straight away, now. All right?'

'Whatever you say, my dear,' said Uncle Edward, as she put down the phone.

Trent was standing at the far end of the passage when she emerged from the telephone room. He took one look at her face and said, 'Bad news?'

'It's Joe,' she said, not stopping. 'He's very ill in hospital in Mexico City. I've got to get to him as soon as I possibly can.'

She walked quickly through the restaurant, with Trent beside her.

At the outside door into the street she paused and turned to him. 'Thanks for the lunch,' she said briefly. 'Goodbye, Mr Marston.' She just wanted to get away. Trent Marston was the last man she wanted with her just now, He wouldn't even begin to understand her feelings for Joe. To him Joe Kent would merely be the sales manager—a cog in the wheel of the business, and a rather weak cog at that.

But he was still beside her as she hurried along the crowded pavement. 'Where are you going?' he asked.

Anywhere, away from you, she almost said. But better counsel prevailed. 'To the travel agents, to see if they can book me a flight,' she told him briefly, dodging around a fat lady with two shopping bags.

She felt his hand close over her arm, stopping her by its steely strength. 'Hold on a minute,' he said, 'I've got a better idea. I have a tame travel man in London who could probably do better for you, much more rapidly, than a local firm. Let's go back to the office and I'll do some phoning straight away.'

Emma hesitated only a moment. What he said made sense; he would probably command much better service than she could. And her need to get to Joe made her private feud with Trent Marston sink into insignificance. 'Thank you,' she said.

He hadn't waited for her to agree; already they were halfway to the car park. This was a man who moved rapidly when action was necessary.

Half an hour later, in the office, he put down the phone with a satisfied grunt. 'There you are,' he said. 'Tomorrow. I couldn't get a direct flight. It's PanAmerican via Houston, but it shouldn't make all that much difference in time. Okay? It means travelling up to London tonight—can you manage that?'

'Yes, of course. And—thank you, you've been very helpful.' She hadn't really been listening to his efforts on the phone, she had been too busy thinking about dear old Joe, all alone and desperately ill in a hospital thousands of miles away. 'I'll get home now and pack.'

He got to his feet. 'We may as well drive back together. You can leave your car here for Malcolm to pick up later.'

She said, passing a hand vaguely across her forehead. 'No, please, there's no need for you to come.'

He smiled faintly. 'But I have to pack too,' he said.

'You're going back to London?' she asked mechanically.

He thrust some papers into a leather briefcase, and closed the desk drawers. 'I'm coming with you, to Mexico. Tomorrow,' he said, and led her firmly out of the office.

CHAPTER FIVE

'WELCOME to Mexico City,' said Trent, as the limousine he had hired at the airport jolted its stop-go progress, wedged into the solid, panting chaos of traffic. 'The biggest, untidiest and most fascinating city in the world.'

Emma looked out of the car window, but could see very little over the tops of the cars that surrounded them: crumbling ancient buildings between towering modern blocks, tall trees, the domes of churches, all covered by a haze of urban smog.

She looked, but she hardly registered anything. She was desperately tired, after a flight that seemed never-ending, and she was desperately worried about Joe. It had been maddening to be stuck up in an aeroplane not able to make contact, or get news of him, for all those hours, but now that the end was in sight she felt worse than ever, with a sick stomach-turning fear of what might be waiting just ahead.

She turned to Trent, sitting back urbane and composed, as he had been on the whole of the journey, and felt a quick stab of anger that he should be so unconcerned. But of course Joe was nothing to him. It would even relieve him of a few problems if Joe—if Joe—— She choked, and swallowed hard.

'Is it—is it much farther to the hospital?' The car had come to a complete halt now, in the middle of a colossal traffic jam.

She was lacing her fingers together, looking pleadingly up at him, and suddenly he leaned forward and she felt the warmth and strength of his hands covering hers. 'Relax, Emma.' His voice was so kind that she hardly recognised it. 'Don't *worry*, it won't do any good and you're tired. Joe will be having the best possible attention. We are very proud of our hospitals in Mexico.'

Surprise jerked her out of her fear about Joe. 'We?' she queried, deliberately trying to let go of her worry.

'Yes—we. In case it interests you, I happen to be one quarter Mexican myself. My grandfather, my mother's father, was Mexican. Spanish Mexican, I mean. We can't claim descent from the Maya or the Aztecs, or any of the other colourful tribes who were around these parts in the beginning. I often wish we could. They were fascinating.'

Emma's knowledge of Mexican history was decidedly sketchy, but she had seen TV films, read bits here and there, and she had a chilling picture in her mind of bloody sacrifices to horrifying animal gods.

'Oh, but weren't they terribly cruel and inhuman?'

Trent shrugged. 'The Spanish who conquered them in the end weren't exactly men of sweetness and light either. The Aztecs fought like tigers—but the Spaniards had the guns. That's life.'

She glanced up at the hard face of the man sitting beside her—the brown skin drawn tightly over high, proud cheekbones, the chiselled lips, the imperious tilt of the dark head. Oh yes, she could see the Spanish conquistador in him. It would explain a lot. *The Spanish had the guns.* In any sort of fight he would have the guns; he would win because he had everything it took to win; he had, to an almost ridiculous degree, what his own Spanish ancestors must have had—that superb arrogance that knew it couldn't lose.

That was why she had to get away from him and stay away. Because if it came to a fight—about business matters or—or anything else, she wasn't going to win.

She said, 'So you're partly at home here?'

'Partly. My grandfather died a few years ago, but my American grandmother is still alive and well and

living in Mexico. She has relatives in the U.S. who
would like her to go back there, but she refuses to
move. She loves the house where she's lived all these
years and her garden is her pride and joy and she likes
to show it off to visitors. I must take you to meet her
while we're here.'

Emma murmured something non-committal. She
had to admit that she had been grateful for Trent's
help on the journey, and his knowledge of this huge,
confusing city was taking a load from her, but she
didn't intend that her gratitude should include accept-
ing any friendly overtures from him, outside business.
Obviously, it suited him now to be friends, in order to
erase from her memory that scene with Lisa that she
had overheard.

'So you came along with me so that you could visit
your grandmother?' said Emma. She hoped that wasn't
wishful thinking. If he said Yes, then she could get
away from him very soon. She could book in at the
hotel where Joe had been staying, could visit Joe each
day, and take things from there. At least she would be
rid of Trent Marston's disturbing company, and she
was sure she could manage the language problem quite
satisfactorily.

His narrowed dark eyes fixed themselves on her—
glinting, curious. 'And what,' he said, 'is that supposed
to mean?'

'Mean? What should it mean, except what I said?'
Her voice sounded squeaky. When he looked at her
like that it did odd things to her breathing.

He leaned back, crossing one long leg over the other.
'Merely that I find women have a way of asking leading
questions.'

'Well, that wasn't one,' she said crossly. But of
course it had been, and he knew it. Damn the man, he
was far too perceptive for any little ploy of hers to
work. He saw through it immediately. 'I merely asked
you if the reason you came with me was so that you

could visit your grandmother,' she said again. 'Was it?'

She looked out of the window at the mass of completely stationary cars, but she seemed to feel Trent's gaze on the back of her head.

'No,' he said.

The single, enigmatic word, and the tone he said it in, made her swing round to face him, a question in her eyes. He hadn't travelled all this way because of Joe—he didn't know Joe. He couldn't be taking up the reins of business because there wasn't any particular business going on here—only a couple of visits planned to look round a trade exhibition in the hope of making contacts. So if he hadn't come to visit his relatives, then why *had* he come? For the first time the question occurred to her, and it surprised her that she hadn't thought of it before.

Had he come because he wanted—for some unknown reason—to be with her? And if he had, what did he expect to get out of it? Posed starkly like that, the question made her heart begin to beat heavily.

Whatever the answer, he wasn't telling her. His eyes met hers, narrowed mockingly, his mouth twitched at the corners. Oh yes, he would enjoy keeping her guessing; that was all part of the power game he was so expert in. She turned away, biting her lip in annoyance.

The big car revved up. Outside the window she saw the traffic begin to move again, apparently in all directions. Trent crossed two fingers with a grin and said, 'We should make it this time. We've only a few kilometres to go now.' And the words brought back Emma's worries about Joe, blotting out everything else.

The hospital was huge, bewildering, in line with everything else she had so far seen in Mexico, but Trent seemed to know his way around and she followed him to where a pretty, dark-skinned girl sat behind a reception desk. He, naturally, spoke perfect Spanish.

Emma could follow most of it if she concentrated hard. She might possibly have got by on her own here. But again she was glad that Trent was with her. Just at first, just until she felt less worked up and could cope again.

He leaned on the polished desk, conducting his enquiries without haste. The girl smiled back at him with eyes as sloe-dark as his own as she answered his queries. She was aware of him, enjoying even this briefest encounter with a man who looked as fabulous as Trent Marston.

Finally he straightened up. '*Muchas gracias, señorita. Es usted muy agradable.*'

Again that exchange of smiles. Come on, thought Emma frantically. Come *on*! Cut out all the flowery exchange of Spanish courtesies. Her anxiety was swamping her now, she felt sick with nerves and impatience.

She grabbed Trent's arm as he led her along corridors to a waiting area with comfortable seats. 'Is he all right? How is he? Did she say?'

He pushed her gently on to a bench seat and sat down beside her, putting one arm round her shoulders. 'Ssh, Emma, just wait a bit longer. There'll be someone coming soon and then we'll know.'

His arm felt strong and comforting and suddenly she wanted to lean against him and bury her head against his shoulder. But that was weak and silly. She sat up stiffly, fixing her gaze on the tiled wall opposite.

A nurse appeared, then a young doctor. Trent stood talking to them quickly in Spanish, but Emma sat where she was. She couldn't bear to listen, even if she could have understood their rapid speech. And after one look at their grave faces she couldn't even bear to look. It was going to be the worst—she knew it was. She felt cold and heavy all through her body, as if her limbs had turned to concrete.

At last Trent slipped back on to the seat beside her

and she saw that the nurse and the doctor had gone. 'Emma,' said Trent gently. She made herself look up.

'He's going to be all right,' Trent said.

She stared at him with glazed eyes. She had been so sure that Joe was dead.

'You m-mean——'

'He's going to be all right,' he said again, firmly this time. 'He had a coronary attack—not too severe. Fortunately he was in the dining room of his hotel when it happened and they managed to get him in here straight away. They say he's responding well to treatment. The Sister says she will tell him that you're here, but she would much prefer you to wait until tomorrow before you see him. Unless, that is, you insist. She thinks it would be better for him not to be disturbed in any way—even pleasantly—today.'

Emma drew in a long, shaky breath. 'Whatever's best for Joe——' She began to shiver. 'I thought—I thought——' Tears welled up and ran slowly down her cheeks and she didn't know until she tasted the salt in her mouth. 'Oh dear,' she whispered, 'I was so frightened——'

'Yes,' said Trent. 'I know you were.' His arm was round her, bracing her. 'Now, come along, you don't want to stay here. You need a good meal—you hardly pecked at anything on the plane. Then a good sleep and Emma will have her usual fighting spirit back again by the morning.' He wiped her cheeks with a folded handkerchief and yanked her to her feet. She wondered dimly if he had a sister; he would have made a nice older brother.

She had to leave everything to him. Her head was aching and she felt as if she were running a slight temperature. The air was cool outside, and she couldn't stop her teeth chattering. She stayed close to Trent while he found a taxi, which deposited them at what she vaguely realised was a very plushy hotel. After a short interlude at the reception desk they were wafted silently upwards and ushered into a suite of rooms that appeared to be almost a self-contained apartment. The uniformed boy put down Emma's slim hand-travel case at the bottom of the wide bed and departed, grinning widely as he slipped a tip into his breast-pocket.

She sank down wearily into the softness of the bed. Trent leaned over her and put a hand on her forehead. 'Into bed with you,' he said. He opened her case and rummaged in it, finally throwing a pale blue nylon nightie towards her. 'Very chic!' he grinned. 'Now get into it.'

When she didn't obey he came and towered over her. 'Do you want me to undress you?' he growled.

'Go away,' said Emma feebly.

He looked down at her without smiling. 'Another time, perhaps?' he said, and he might have been joking or he might not. In her hazy state she wasn't sure.

This was the moment to make it quite plain to him that her gratitude for his help was not going to extend to making herself available, if that was what he had in mind. She had never had a love affair, simply because she had never been in love—although Jim Bolton, and others, had had ideas in that direction from time to time. To fall for a man like Trent Marston would be about as clever as jumping into a bonfire with firecrackers exploding round you. You'd be lucky to get out alive, and even if you did you would be scarred for life.

But at this moment she couldn't think of any way to put it so that he would get the message plain and clear, and before she managed to speak he had disappeared through a door on the other side of the room.

He came back with a glass and two white tablets. 'Take these,' he said. 'They're only asprins, and the water should be okay at this hotel.'

He waited until she had swallowed the tablets and then turned to the door. 'I'll go and see about food. Any special preferences?'

'I'm not hungry,' she muttered, letting her head sink on to the pillow. It was beautifully cool and smooth.

Trent walked back to the bed and stood, frowning. 'Do you feel really ill, Emma? Should I get a doctor?'

'No—please. I'm—just tired——' She closed her eyes. All of a sudden she felt completely limp as if her bones had melted. This must be jet-lag, she thought, like having gas at the dentist's when everything gets indistinct.

She knew vaguely that he pulled off the jacket of her lightweight suit, she felt his hands at the fastening of her skirt, knew that he was lifting her legs on to the bed. It seemed quite a natural thing to be happening. She closed her eyes and heaved a sigh of contentment as she sank into the softness of the bed. She heard him murmur something that sounded like 'Sleep well, sweetheart,' and she felt his lips brush lightly against her forehead, but it might not have happened. She might have been dreaming by then, for almost immediately she was asleep.

Time became eclipsed. The next thing she knew she was falling, falling, clutching at nothing, trying to cry out but making no sound. She opened her eyes, choking and gasping, to find Trent patting her cheek.

'My word, you have got yourself into a state,' he observed.

She stared at him glassily. 'I—I was having a nightmare.'

'So I gathered. I thought it wise to pull you out of it.'

Emma dragged herself up, blinking. The heavy brocade curtains were closed and the bedside light switched on. It had been daylight when she went to asleep.

'What time is it?' she said.

'Time to eat,' said Trent. 'I'm famished. I waited for you to wake up. Would you like to eat in bed, or do you feel up to getting dressed?'

'I'll get up,' she said quickly. She felt very—vulnerable, lying here with him standing beside the bed. 'Can you give me ten minutes?'

He nodded. 'Not a second more. I'll ring down and tell them to bring it up.'

As soon as he had gone and the door was firmly closed Emma slithered out of bed. Her headache had gone and her face felt cool. She decided she wasn't running a temperature. She took a quick shower in the adjoining bathroom and splashed herself from the bottle of cologne on the glass shelf. There were other bottles—after-shave, bath crystals, roll-on, talc. This must be a very expensive hotel indeed; certainly not one that she could afford to patronise. She would have to get that settled with Trent as soon as possible; just for the moment, though, she would enjoy the luxury.

She went back into the bedroom. She would have to wear again the lightweight beige suit and patterned blouse she had worn for travelling, because she hadn't any other outer clothes with her. It hadn't seemed worth the hassle of taking anything heavier than hand-baggage on the plane with her, when everything she would need was already here, in Mexico, in Joe's keeping. It would still be at his hotel, she supposed, and she would go along there later on and make arrangements about it. Perhaps she could take on the room he had so abruptly had to vacate, if it hadn't already been re-let. She had the address of the hotel written in her diary, and she was sure it would be a much more modest place than this multi-star palace she was in at present, and more within her means.

She took clean bra and briefs from her case and looked round for her blouse. It was draped carefully on a hanger, hitched on to the knob of the closet door. The jacket of the suit was hanging over the back of one chair, the skirt over another.

Her cheeks flamed. 'Shall I undress you?' Trent had said, and he must have done just that, for she had certainly been in no state to dispose so neatly of her clothes. Hazily she remembered his hands at the waist-band of her skirt and then it had seemed almost natural, nothing to worry about or resist. At least he hadn't gone to the extreme of stripping her completely and putting her into the blue nylon nightie, which still lay across the bottom of the bed.

She dressed hastily, telling herself she was stupid to let it bother her. He must have had plenty of practice in undressing girls—although in different circumstances—and it wouldn't mean a thing to him. She would put it right out of her mind.

She took her make-up box from her case and did her face carefully, steadying her hand to apply beige eye-shadow, brushing on extra mascara, combing her dark gold hair back from her face and into a loose knot in her neck. She wasn't going to face Trent looking less than her best, after the way she had gone to bits in the hospital, and afterwards. She had to show him that she wasn't usually a helpless female, ready to submit to his masculine dominance.

She stood up and walked to the door that led to the adjoining room. She would begin, she decided, by in-sisting on moving out of this palace of a hotel into something more within the Fairley Brothers budget, and she would simply ignore any pressure he put on her to change her mind. She paused for a moment, her fingers on the door-knob. Then, with her smooth dark gold head held well up, and determined to ignore the nervous fluttering in her stomach, she opened the door.

The room she entered was vast and shadowy, lit only by a crystal chandelier lamp pulled down low over a table at one end. The table was laid immaculately for a meal, with gleaming silver and glass, and a white-coated waiter moved silently between the table and a high trolley. A mouthwatering savoury smell issued from beneath the covered dishes he was carrying.

Trent emerged from the shadows on the far side of the room and came towards her. 'Well done, only thirty seconds late.' There was a smile in his voice. He looked devastating in dark, fitting trousers and a white silk shirt. He pulled out a chair for her at the table and sat down opposite. The waiter poured the regulation amount of sparkling wine from a cradle clinking with ice into Trent's glass. He sipped it and nodded. Both their glasses were filled.

This, thought Emma, was VIP treatment indeed: a private suite in a luxury hotel; a superb meal served in one's own room; champagne on ice. A very far cry from her recent travels with Joe, but oh, how she wished she could be back with him again at a hot-dog stand in New York, as they drank Coke and laughed together to keep their spirits up.

The waiter hovered. 'Will that be all, sir?'

'Thank you, yes, we'll look after ourselves now.' Trent dismissed the waiter with a smile; a moment later the door closed silently behind him and they were alone.

Trent lifted the lid of his soup bowl and sniffed. 'Smells good—they do you very well here, I've stayed here before. I ordered a duck thing to follow the soup, I hope that meets with your approval.'

Emma murmured something inaudible. The smell of the soup was tantalising, and the 'duck thing' sounded delicious. She just wished that Trent Marston wasn't sitting on the other side of the table, smiling at her under those long, dark lashes of his.

He lifted his glass. 'Let's drink to the success of our new venture. Fairley Brothers Mark Two. Or Fairley and Marston, what do you think?'

'I prefer the first,' she said stiffly, taking a sip of her wine.

'I see. You disapprove of the Marston touch?'

She shrugged. 'I'm not interested.' She told herself she didn't care what he called the new firm. She wouldn't let him see that he had touched her on the raw with his blithe suggestion of a new name. It had been Fairley Brothers when her father was alive and it had stayed Fairley Brothers all the years since. If his name were taken out of the firm's title now it would be like losing him all over again.

'But you *are* interested in seeing the firm re-vitalised?'

'Of course I am, you know that.'

'That's all I wanted to know,' he said. 'Then let's drink to Fairley Brothers, if that's the name you prefer.'

Emma glanced at him suspiciously. He was being too thoughtful, too pleasant—it didn't ring true. He was manipulating her, just to get something he wanted, and she wished she knew exactly what it was, because she didn't trust him for one moment.

She lifted her glass and drank deeply of the bubbly, delightfully cool wine and felt marginally more relaxed. She would allow herself to drink just enough to quieten her nerves but be careful not to overdo it. Not with this disturbingly magnetic man sitting across the table looking at her in a way that made her heart beat unevenly.

'You look very charming, Emma.' His voice was deep and velvety; his long dark lashes brushed his cheeks. 'That colour suits you.'

She put her glass down with a sharp click. 'Thank you very much,' she said briskly. She touched the cuff of her blouse. 'As a matter of fact this suit is all I have here, I must go to Joe's hotel tomorrow and take over the rest of my clothes that I left with him when I came home for Lisa's wedding at rather short notice.' She looked levelly across the table at him. 'And I thought it would be a good idea if I took over his room as well. This hotel isn't in my price range.'

His brows went up and he didn't look seductive any longer, he looked annoyed. But he said evenly, 'What's the name of Joe's hotel? Do you know where it is?'

She rummaged in her handbag, which was lying beside her chair, and found her diary. 'I wrote it down when we made the booking. I had a room booked for myself, but that was cancelled. Yes, here it is—Hotel Redonda.'

His brows lifted even further. 'Yes, I know it, it's on Insurgentes. Clean and cheap. I think we shall stay here for the moment. I have business contacts in Mexico, and a good address is essential. One of the first rules of business is to look prosperous.'

'I'm sure you're right,' she said very coolly. 'Well, you can stay here and look prosperous and I'll take over Joe's room at——'

'Oh no, you won't,' he broke in. 'I should never be able to face your uncle if I let you stay in this wicked city on your own.'

'So *that's* why you came with me?' she heard herself say. 'Because Uncle Edward put me in your charge?'

His maddeningly enigmatic smile appeared again. 'Why are you so anxious to find out my motives for coming? Would you believe me if I told you that I'd fallen madly in love with you at first sight? That when I saw you standing in the church porch in that wispy green dress, with the organ playing in the background it put all sorts of thoughts into my mind? Such as sirens sitting on rocks, their music luring hapless sailors to their doom? Would you believe that?'

'Don't be absurd,' she said crossly.

'Well then, I'll have to think up some other reason, won't I?' Trent sighed heavily. 'Meanwhile, our food's waiting.' He leaned across the table and took the lid off her soup bowl. 'There—isn't that inviting?'

It was. Thick and creamy, with croûtons floating on the top and slivers of cucumber. It was supposed to be bad for the digestion to argue and quarrel over a meal, so Emma picked up her spoon and decided to wait until it was finished before she tackled Trent about the things that were bothering her: about staying in this too-expensive hotel; about why he had come with her; most of all about his attitude towards her and what he wanted from her, which was the most puzzling of all and the thought of which made her distinctly uneasy.

She was quite determined to clear everything up—but meanwhile the meal was superb and was there to be enjoyed. 'Tell me about Mexico,' she said.

He smiled at her, that dark, devilish smile. 'Mexico,' he said, 'is a thing to be experienced, rather than talked about. Like love,' he added.

'I don't want to talk about love,' she snapped. She choked a little as she took a sip of soup and found it highly seasoned.

'Too hot for you?' he mocked, and as she met his bland gaze with fury in her eyes, he added, 'The soup, I mean, of course.'

She said with as much dignity as she could muster, 'May we please enjoy our meal without this ridiculous conversation?'

To her disgust he burst out laughing. 'Certainly, if you wish. I was merely trying to lighten the atmosphere a little.' He started on his soup. 'Now then— Mexico. Mexico,' he intoned, 'is a land full of vivid contrasts, beautiful and exotic. The capital, Mexico City, is built upon three layers of civilisation. There are picturesque villages in many different Indian variations, there is art as good as Italy and Spain—and in my biassed opinion better—and archaeology equal to ancient Greece or Egypt. There is sightseeing and entertainment for the visitor. Also a unique culinary tradition.' He paused to drink a spoonful of soup. 'As you have just found out for yourself.'

His mouth twitched, inviting her to laugh, but she wasn't going to laugh with him. She hadn't asked him to come and she had no intention of giving in tamely to his rather too obvious gestures of friendship.

'Very funny,' she said coldly.

After that they ate in silence and Emma began to feel more and more uneasy and embarrassed. She felt a growing anger, too, that he had put her in what she looked upon as a completely false position by being so cagey and enigmatic. She couldn't believe that he had brought her here with a seduction in mind. And yet she didn't know the man at all, really, and what little she did know pointed to the fact that he was a charmer and heartbreaker. He might be the kind of man who would merely think that a girl, alone with him in a strange city, was fair game.

They had reached the coffee stage now. She glanced across at him, at the dark, hard face and the sensual mouth, and remembered how brutal he could be, how he had flayed poor Lisa with his savage words. And yet he could be kind too. He had been kind at the hospital, and when he brought her back here to the hotel. And he could be devastatingly, powerfully attractive. She began to tremble deep inside as she remembered the way he had taken her in his arms and kissed her after the party, and how she had put up no resistance. Worse, how she had kissed him back with a hunger that had shocked her. He had that much physical, masculine potency that had turned her bones to water.

She felt suddenly very young and inexperienced—and afraid.

Slowly he lifted his eyes and met hers, watching him, and she was unable to look away. 'Well?' he said slowly. 'Have you made up your mind?'

'W-what do you mean?' she stammered. 'About what?'

'About me? That's what you were puzzling about, wasn't it? Me and my sinister intentions? How I was planning that we should spend the night?'

Emma felt herself go scarlet, but she kept her head high. Now was the time to learn some more about this man. 'Can you blame me? I have inside information about how you treat women, and it doesn't exactly inspire me with confidence.'

'Oh—we're back to that, are we? You mean your cousin Lisa?'

'Exactly.'

In the short pause that followed her clipped word she didn't take her eyes from his face. Not that it told her anything; he seemed to be able to make his expression completely impassive, to order.

Then he said, 'Yes, I can very well imagine what she told you about me. But try to see it from my point of view—and I think you're fair-minded enough to do so. I see you as a modern young woman, Emma, and intelligent enough to be broad-minded about such things.'

'That's a typical male argument.' She drew down her lips contemptuously. 'I'm certainly intelligent enough to recognise it.'

He shrugged. 'But at least you're not in the least like your cousin. You're not a silly child, full of fantasies about marriages made in heaven, and waiting for the one man in the world, etc., etc.'

'Is that how you see Lisa?' she said, quietly furious.

'More or less. It wouldn't have been so bad if she stopped there. But the trouble was that all that unreleased passion had been building up while she waited for her hero to put in an appearance.' He smiled grimly. 'That was extremely dangerous.'

'Rubbish!' snapped Emma. Lisa was sweet and unawakened certainly (though she hoped Richard would have attended to that by now). But—seething with violent passion? No, never. 'I know Lisa. I've known her all our lives. She isn't like that at all.'

'How would you know?' he said dryly. 'You're not a man.'

They stared at each other, her eyes wide and unbelieving, his darkly mocking.

Then, across the room, a telephone buzzed discreetly. Trent got up to answer it as Emma felt a dreadful stab of fear. Joe—was it Joe, was he worse?

She sprang to her feet, trembling, and then, as she heard Trent's words, sank down again into her chair. 'Who did you say? Royston? Oh yes, I know. Ask Mr Royston to wait, will you? Tell him I'll be right down.' He spoke in English, as he had done to the waiter. This must be an English-speaking hotel—American, perhaps, she registered dimly, through her relief.

Trent replaced the receiver and looked towards Emma. 'An old business acquaintance of mine—an American, living and operating in Mexico. I did some telephoning while you were sleeping earlier on—making contacts. I won't ask him up here, you're too tired to meet strangers tonight. Excuse me, please, Emma, I'll be right back.'

As soon as the door closed behind him Emma jumped up again and switched on all the lights. She must find out what sort of a hotel suite this was, and from that she could guess his intentions. Because if there was only one bedroom—

There *was* only one bedroom, the one she had been asleep in earlier. She went carefully round every door and there was no trace of another. It was evidently a double suite—the one large entertaining room, the one large bedroom, the one large double bed. She stood looking at it, with its patterned cover in vaguely Mexican colours of reds and yellows and blues, and her stomach flipped over painfully.

She put a hand on the door-frame, as if she needed support, and perhaps she did. She had tried to find out Trent Marston's intentions and she had got precisely nowhere. She was stuck here with him, in this hotel suite for two. It was late at night—she glanced at her watch and realised that she had failed to put it back during the flight. It said four minutes past five. That meant it must be about eleven o'clock here; or even twelve, she wasn't sure about the time lag. She passed a hand over her forehead, and her mind felt like cotton wool.

If Trent tried to make love to her she would refuse. And if he insisted or used force she would fight him every inch of the way. She remembered how his kiss had felt and hoped she would be capable of fighting him. Then she remembered Lisa's tears and felt tears begin to gather thickly behind her own eyes. What a horrid muddle it all was!

She stood staring at the patterned bedspread and the colours blurred and ran together before her.

'Attractive, don't you think?' Trent's voice came close to her ear.

Her breath caught in her throat and she jumped in surprise, her heart hammering. He was standing behind her, both hands on her shoulders, holding her with her back to him.

'The bedspread is native work,' he remarked. 'This is an American hotel, but they support local industry, which makes for good relations all round. Were you looking longingly at the bed, thinking of getting back into it?' His voice was teasing.

'No, I wasn't,' she said sharply, 'I've had enough sleep for the moment.' She felt a fool, standing with her back to him, unable to move.

He chuckled softly. 'I wasn't really referring to sleep,' he said. 'But I mustn't put ideas into that lovely golden head of yours, must I?'

'Oh, you—you——' she gasped. 'Let me go!' It was humiliating to be held there like a prisoner.

'Of course,' Trent murmured laughingly, and touched his cheek against her hair. 'If you insist.'

Her back was pressing against the firmness of his chest. Two thin layers of silky material was all that separated their bodies. She could feel the heat from him as if they were both naked. She should have pulled away, but she was totally unable to move.

Swiftly his hands slipped from her shoulders down

to her waist, brushing against her breasts under the
silk of her blouse, lingering there for a fraction of a
second.

He turned her round to face him and his hands
linked themselves behind her waist. 'Do you insist?'
he said softly. '*Do* you, Emma?'

'Yes,' she said breathlessly. 'Yes, I do.' But she
didn't move.

His face was very close to hers now and he was smiling, an odd, satisfied smile. Very slowly his mouth
came down to hers, his lips moving against her own,
setting up an almost painful tingling along her nerves.
Then, with sudden roughness, he claimed her mouth
completely in a long, deeply exciting kiss that went on
and on as their bodies swayed together.

Emma felt as if she were drowning. Madness—madness—was the word that kept running through her
brain. But it was ecstasy as well as madness, and the
blending of the two set up such a violence of desire in
her that she could do nothing but respond to him,
clinging to him in a kind of frenzy, glorying in the
new, delicious sensations that he was deliberately setting up in her.

Then into her rocking consciousness came again the
memory of his voice, cold and vicious, saying, 'Shut
up, you stupid little fool, and pull yourself together. I
don't give a damn for you, Lisa, I never did.'

With a little groan she pulled herself out of his arms.
'Stop it!' she cried raggedly. 'Stop it, I'm not a vulnerable teenager for you to practise your technique on!'

He recoiled and she saw that just for a moment she
had pierced his guard. 'Is that what you think I was
doing?' His eyes glittered like polished jet. There was
no teasing smile now, no lightness in his voice. He
looked as his noble Spanish ancestors must have looked
if they had suffered an insult, and she felt a sudden
qualm of fear and stumbled away from him.

He came after her and gripped her wrist, not

brutally, but so that she couldn't pull away. 'Tell me, Emma, is that what you thought?'

'What else can I think? You won't tell me anything. I don't understand why you felt you had to come to Mexico with me, if it isn't to visit your relatives here. I could perfectly well have managed on my own. I don't understand why you booked this suite with only one bedroom. It seems obvious that you believe I'll let you make love to me. What else can I think?' she finished rather wildly.

She shook her head in desperate confusion and a strand of silky dark gold hair escaped and fell across her temple. Trent put out a hand and very gently smoothed it back, staring into her face for a long moment. Then he said, 'Come and sit down. I didn't think that talking was necessary, but I'd forgotten that women have to have everything explained.'

He drew her back into the sitting-room and pulled her down beside him into a deep crimson velvet sofa. 'Now,' he said, 'what were your questions? Ah yes, why did I come to Mexico with you? Several reasons, one of which was to take up the job where the firm's marketing manager, your friend Joe, had unfortunately to put it down. I wanted to find out exactly what the order-book looked like. Also, I had the idea that I might be of some small service to you.' He slid her an ironic smile. 'It appears that I was mistaken.'

Emma didn't rise to that one. He was trying to make her feel ungracious and put her in the wrong.

He leaned back in the corner of the sofa, long legs crossed nonchalantly, the picture of a man completely in control of himself and events. When she didn't comment he went on wryly, 'I thought we could be— friends. As I'm to be an integral part of Fairley Brothers, and as I know the firm means a lot to you, it seemed a pity for there to be bad feeling between us.'

'And you thought that by putting on your super-macho act you could win my friendship after—after what I know about you and your winning ways?' Her tone was supremely contemptuous.

He leaned towards her and slid a hand along the back of the sofa, not touching her, but close enough for her to sense the vibrant warmth of his fingers behind her neck, setting up an answering vibration deep inside her. But she couldn't move away.

'I think,' he said softly, his mouth close to her hair, 'that I could make you forget you ever heard that damned conversation at the wedding reception.'

'*No!*' She shook her head violently.

He withdrew his hand and sat back again, smiling faintly. 'We shall see. As for your other question—I took this suite as it was the only one they had vacant. I shall be quite comfortable sleeping in here on this sofa. That was my intention.'

'I don't believe you,' she said flatly. 'You were trying to——'

'Use my wonderful technique to persuade you to share the bed with me? Oh no, my dear Emma, you're wrong there. That was never my intention. Although I admit to getting a little carried away just now. You're a very lovely and desirable young woman, you know.'

'I suppose desirable young women are two a penny to you?' she said childishly.

He laughed and shook his head. 'Much more valuable than that. Let's say——' he looked up at the ceiling '—two for ten new pence.'

'Oh, you're intolerable!' she burst out. If she had been standing up she would have stamped her foot.

'So you keep on telling me,' he said mildly. 'Now, let's put an end to this fruitless conversation and have a drink together and talk about something we can agree upon.'

'Such as——?' she questioned coldly.

'Business, of course.' He smiled into her eyes, and anything less businesslike than his smile she couldn't imagine. 'That's primarily why I'm here, didn't I mention that before?'

He got up and poured out two drinks. 'This is
definitely non-alcoholic,' he said, handing her a tall
glass with ice clinking in its pale green contents. 'Lime
and lemon—very innocuous. So that you can't harbour
any more dark suspicions about my motives.'

Emma sipped her drink; it was cool and refreshing
and she felt calmer straight away. 'Before we start to
talk business,' she said, 'perhaps we could ring the
hospital and check on Joe's condition, and what time I
may visit him tomorrow?'

'Certainly, I'll do that.' He sprang to his feet and
went across to the telephone. The call came through
quickly and he made his enquiries, speaking in Spanish
now. Emma watched his face, turned half away from
her as he sat at the writing desk. Against the background of the long crimson brocade curtains, his brown
skin and black hair, with the thick, upward-sweeping
brows and sharply etched features, gave him a devilish
look. For all his light talk since they had arrived here,
he would be a dangerous man to provoke. She had
witnessed his anger once and she had no intention of
being the target for it herself. But neither would she
allow him to dominate her.

As she listened to him, it occurred to her that she
had better let him know that she understood the language herself. It might convince him that she was quite
capable of looking after herself and finding her own
way around.

Trent put down the receiver and looked across to
her. 'Joe's improvement is being maintained and they
say you may visit tomorrow morning from eleven
o'clock.'

Her face lit up. 'Oh good, that's terrific.'

He was very still, watching her. 'Yes, it is, isn't it?'
he said quietly, and he sounded as if he really meant it.
He was full of surprises, wasn't he? Emma thought a
little ungraciously. For some reason she was peeved

that he should be glad about Joe's recovery. It would be so much better if she could go on hating him—better, and safer.

'Mind if I put through a personal call while I'm here?' he asked, and she said, 'No, of course not,' and started to get up to go into the bedroom and leave him to it, but he waved her back to the sofa again.

She picked up a magazine from the low table beside the sofa, but even though she wasn't looking at him she was conscious that he was sitting forward impatiently, fingers drumming on the desk.

His call came through and he relaxed back into his chair, crossing his legs. 'Juanita? Ah—at last! Where on earth have you been all day—I've tried to get you at least three times since we arrived?' A deep chuckle. 'Yes—we. I have a business colleague with me. Nobody you know.' Another chuckle. 'No. A lovely lady, as a matter of fact.'

Emma had a very curious feeling. Suddenly she didn't want to hear any more. Juanita was no doubt one of the desirable young women that he priced at two for ten new pence, a dark, voluptuous Spanish beauty. She could almost see her at the other end of the line, lying among vivid cushions, cradling the telephone receiver against her smooth cheek, pouting her resentment. Trent Marston would enjoy playing off one girl against another. He really was a bastard, she thought, her anger rising.

She glared at the pictures in the magazine, seeing nothing. 'Tonight? Now?' he was saying. 'Wouldn't it be——? Yes, of course I do, you know that. Right, if you say so—I'll get a taxi and be with you in no time. *Hasta leugo, querida.*'

He replaced the receiver, looking very pleased with life. 'Well, that's that,' he said in a satisfied way. 'You won't mind if I leave you now?'

She lifted her eyes from the magazine. 'Of course not,' she said coolly.

He went towards the door. 'I'll be back here early and we can breakfast together, then I'll take you along to the hospital.'

She shrugged. 'Don't hurry. I can manage quite well by myself.'

'Of course you can't,' he said sharply. He hesitated and came back to stand before her. 'Promise you'll wait for me.'

Emma glanced up indifferently. 'If you wish.'

He grinned. 'At least you can be sure of having the bed to yourself, 'he said. 'That will be a great relief to you.'

She made no sign of having heard him and he walked to the door again. 'Goodnight, Emma,' he said.

She looked across the room at him. '*Buenas noches, señor,*' she replied with her pretty, well-practised accent.

He checked in sudden surprise, holding the door half open as if he were about to speak, and Emma had a moment of small triumph. Two can play at the game of keeping things to themselves.

But as he closed the door behind him without speaking, her pleasure evaporated. And although she was tired, she lay alone in the big bed for a long time, chasing sleep in vain.

CHAPTER SIX

FROM a long distance away Emma was aware of a burring sound. It stopped and started again three times before she managed to throw out an arm to the bedside telephone. It seemed that she had only slept for five minutes, and it was agony to drag herself awake.

'Your seven o'clock call, madam. Good morning, it's a beautiful day,' said a feminine voice, noticeably Spanish but with an American accent.

'Oh—oh, thank you,' mumbled Emma, blindly feeling the receiver back to its stand.

She turned on to her back and lay there, her eyelids heavy, her tumbled hair spread on the white pillow like a golden aureole, fighting against the temptation to turn over and go back to sleep again, knowing there were things she had to do early this morning, while she was alone, but not quite recalling what they were.

It took an enormous effort, but eventually she dragged herself out of bed and pulled back the velvet curtains, letting the morning sunlight flood into the room. A long way below traffic was already filling the wide thoroughfare; in fact, she was dimly aware that the noise hadn't ceased all night. She looked down at the tops of cars and vans and buses, streaming in both directions, separated by an avenue of trees along the centre of the street. She must be on about the tenth or eleventh floor, she reckoned, but she remembered very little about arriving yesterday, and she hadn't been out of the suite since.

In the bathroom she turned the shower to *Cool* and wakened up rapidly as the water sluiced over her body. Towelling herself, she gathered her thoughts together, remembering all that had happened, dwelling happily

on the heartwarming news that Joe was making good
progress and that she would see him today. That was
the important thing—all that mattered, really—and it
was annoying how memories of Trent Marston came
creeping in all the time. Still, she knew more or less
where she was with him now.

She even knew why he had insisted on coming to
Mexico with her. His reason was quite plain, and it was
called Juanita. It had been explicit in the tone of his
voice as he said '*Hasta luego, querida,*' in that intimate
way. He couldn't wait to see this Juanita, could he?

Why he couldn't have told her straight out that he
had a girl-friend in Mexico she couldn't imagine.
Probably he had thought she would bring up the subject of Lisa again, and however he pretended to the
contrary, he must feel guilty about that.

She dressed in the beige travelling suit again and put
the short jacket over her blouse. She really must go to
the Hotel Redonda and pick up the rest of her luggage
at the earliest possible moment. She hated having to
wear the same clothes day after day.

She did her make-up carefully and brushed her hair
loosely. That was another thing she must do today—
get a shampoo. After tossing and turning in bed last
night it looked to her far from its usual shiny self.

When she was ready she went out on to the thickly-
carpeted landing. 'We'll breakfast together,' she remembered Trent saying before he left her last night to
go to that—that girl, Juanita. He hadn't mentioned a
time, she didn't think. Well, he could look for her when
he arrived. She certainly wasn't going to sit up here
like an obedient child in the nursery, waiting for him
to come and summon her downstairs.

She found a lift and was swished down to the ground
floor. As she had guessed, the hotel was an enormous
palace of luxury. In most of the places where she and
Joe had stayed on their tour, if you came down early in
the morning you were greeted by trailing flexes of

vacuum cleaners and sleepy maids with dusters and armsful of bed-linen. But here—although it was only just after eight o'clock—all was fresh and sparkling. The ankle-deep carpets were speckless and the staff was already assembling behind the numerous polished counters in the huge lobby, where even the palms in their tubs looked as if they had had a morning sponge-down.

Emma wandered round until she found what she was looking for—a street map of the city, hanging on a side wall. She remembered that Trent had said that the Hotel Redonda was on Insurgentes. Was that a street, or a square, or what? Yes, here it was, just north of the University. But it seemed to run for miles, right across the city. She would have to enlist the help of a taxi-driver, as soon as she could contrive to get away from Trent. She had a firm intention of managing on her own and not relying on him for everything.

A book-and-magazine stall was open and she bought a guide-book of the city, which would be useful when she was finding her way about alone. She also found out where to change her supply of banknotes into pesos, for her small expenses. The traveller's cheques she still possessed from her tour with Joe would meet any larger demands.

The big lobby was still comparatively empty, although a few early risers were drifting about, and travel-weary new arrivals, in ones and twos, kept appearing from the direction of the huge plate-glass doors, followed by uniformed porters carrying their luggage.

Emma sat down in a corner, in a lounge seat under a tall palm, to consult her guide-book and wait for the *cambio* counter to open at nine o'clock when she could change her money and find the most likely snack-bar in the hotel to get some breakfast.

She tried to concentrate on the guide-book, but at the back of her mind, like a storm-cloud rising, was the thought that Trent Marston would be arriving soon—coming straight from his lovely girl-friend Juanita. By this time the picture of her had become so vivid to Emma that it was almost as if she had actually seen her—seen them together all night in some satin-cushioned bed. It was no good trying to tell herself that it didn't matter a hoot to her where Trent Marston spent his nights. It seemed that the man had got under her skin to such an extent that she was aware of him even when he wasn't there.

But he *was* there. She sensed his presence before she saw him, and looked up to see him striding purposefully across the wide expanse of the lobby, threading his way between the empty tables and lounge chairs, looking disgustingly handsome in a cinnamon brown suit and a cream shirt, his black hair gleaming. Immaculately groomed, impeccably shaved. Evidently he kept a supply of clothes and toilet articles at Juanita's address, wherever that was, for he had taken nothing with him when he left the hotel last night. That figured, she thought scathingly, dredging up her dislike for him.

Then, as he got nearer, he smiled and quickened his step, and her heart gave a sickening lurch and started to thud like a road-drill. It was too ridiculous for words, she told herself vexedly. She would *not* allow him to have this impact on her. It was just his physical presence, of course; charisma was the word, she supposed. 'He makes my knees go wobbly when he just looks at me,' poor Lisa had written. Oh yes, he was a danger to woman—a man to avoid.

She just had time to compose her features into a cool mask before he reached her.

'Good morning, Emma, you're up and about early. I thought I should have to come and rout you out of bed.' He slipped into a chair beside her.

'Good morning, Mr Marston,' she said, ignoring the last bit.

'Sleep well?'

'Very well, thank you.'

He gave her a sideways look. 'Good. So did I.' He was smiling his enigmatic smile—the devil! He knew what she was thinking, of course he did. He had been deliberately devious last night; knowing all the time that he intended to spend the night with Juanita, but purposely leading her on to think he had planned a big seduction scene at the hotel. Why? Just to make her feel foolish, was the only reason she could think of. It must amuse him to draw a response from a girl and then step back. That was exactly how he had treated Lisa, she reminded herself. Well, there won't be another time with me, Mr Trent Marston!

'I was just waiting to change some sterling into pesos,' she said. 'I shall need some small change for taxis and hair-do's and so on.'

He glanced at his watch. 'A bit too early yet. Let's have breakfast first. What do you feel like—rolls and coffee, or *desayuno* with all the trimmings?' His use of the Spanish word for breakfast referred her back quite deliberately to the moment they parted last night, as did the gleam in his dark eyes.

'Rolls and coffee, please,' she said, and then—speaking as deliberately as he had done—'*Quiero bolillo y café, por favor, señor.*'

He grinned. 'Very prettily said. You will now be able to tell me how much you dislike me in two languages, instead of one.'

Once again he seemed to be challenging her to smile and relax and be friends. She glanced up at him, his mouth curved into a coaxing smile, his eyes dark and laughing, and she found herself suddenly wanting to smile back, to talk to him and find out how much they had in common, if they shared the same sense of the ridiculous. She had a feeling that he could be tremendous fun to be with, and that if things had been different he would be a fascinating companion. What utter madness—this man was her enemy still, as he had been from the beginning. It was no doubt because he had spent the night with Juanita that he was so bright and breezy and pleased with himself.

She got to her feet. 'Shall we have breakfast, then?' she said coldly.

The smile left his face and he shrugged. 'As you wish,' he said, and led the way to the nearest coffee bar.

'The doctor is with Señor Kent at present,' said the pretty nurse with the soft voice. She spoke to them both, but her eyes rested on Trent. 'If you will please wait here——'.

Emma's knees were weak as she sank into the seat indicated. Now that the moment had come that she had travelled thousands of miles for, she felt very nervous indeed about what she would see when she was finally allowed to walk through that closed door before her.

Trent stood beside her, frowning slightly. 'Look, Emma, would you mind if I left you here for a short time? This man Royston, who I saw briefly at the hotel yesterday—I promised to look in at his office at the first moment I could, and this seems a good time. He might be very useful to us, he has connections all over Mexico.'

Emma nodded. 'Of course I don't mind,' she said in a surprised tone that seemed to imply that she couldn't care less where he went.

He still didn't move. 'You will want to see Joe on your own, in any case, you won't want me there. And when they turn you out will you wait here for me, if you're ready first?'

'You go ahead and see your friend,' she said, picking up a magazine. 'Go along—you don't have to look after me every second as if I were an idiot child, you know.'

A look of exasperation passed over his face. 'Sometimes I wonder whether you are,' he said, and he turned on his heel and walked away down the long corridor, without a backward look.

Joe was in a small room off the long main ward. Emma's heart was thumping as the nurse took her in to him, but once she saw his face, drawn and pallid, but with the merest trace of his familiar wry grin, she forgot herself and her nervousness and leaned over the high bed to kiss his cheek gently, the tears pricking behind her eyelids. 'Joe darling, what *have* you been getting up to, since I left you on your own? How are you feeling today?'

His eyes seemed to drink in the sight of her. 'Fine,' he said. 'I'm feeling fine, love. Better for seeing you.' He spoke carefully and slowly, without moving his head, but his voice was surprisingly strong.

'I shall come every day to see you,' she promised. 'Is there anything you want, specially?'

His eyes moved to the complicated battery of life-saving apparatus, with its tubes and flasks and dials. 'Not while they have me trussed up like an oven-ready chicken!'

Emma swallowed. Even now Joe could manage to see the funny side of things. 'They'll soon take all this gear off and then you'll be a free-range bird again, you'll see. After that, all you'll have to do is take it easy and rest for a while and you'll be as good as new.'

A little frown squeezed his brows together. 'Emma, love——'

His voice seemed weaker and she knew she mustn't stay or she would tire him. 'Yes, Joe?' She leaned over the bed.

'About the work——' he whispered '——I'm so sorry—I was hoping——'

She put a hand firmly over his limp hand. 'Listen, Joe dear, there's not a thing for you to worry about. Uncle Edward has managed to find a young man to look after things and carry on until you're ready to take over again.' (And may I be forgiven for that white lie; no one was going to take anything over from Trent Marston.) 'He's quite a bright young man—definitely promising—and he's here in Mexico with me, so I'll be able to put him in the picture.'

The frown smoothed out. 'So long as you keep a hand on the reins, Emma, and see that he toes the mark——'

'I will, I promise.' What a fantastic picture *that* presented!

The door opened and a severe-looking Sister appeared. Emma rose immediately and kissed Joe. 'I'll come and see you again very soon, Joe.'

The faintest of grins touched his mouth and he closed his eyes.

As Emma reached the door the Sister murmured, speaking in Spanish, 'Wait outside, please.' She went across to the bed.

A minute or two later she joined Emma in the dorridor. 'Will you please come to my office, *señorita*. Or is it *señora*?' She sat at a desk and motioned Emma to a chair opposite.

'*Señorita*,' Emma told her. 'My name is Fairley. Mr Kent is an old and valued executive in my uncle's company. He has no relatives, and that is why I am here.' She spoke in Spanish.

'Yes, I understand. Now then—he was admitted as an emergency. I understand he is staying at an hotel in Mexico, but unfortunately the clerk on duty omitted to take all the particulars at the time and Señor Kent has not been well enough to question yet. Perhaps you can help me?'

'I think so,' said Emma. 'I have a note of the hotel where he was staying and I shall go there now to do whatever is necessary.'

'Ah—good. Also, we should like to have some personal articles for him, if you will kindly supply those.

Here is a list.' She handed Emma a sheet of paper.

'Certainly, I'll get them as soon as possible and bring them in to you.' Emma stood up, hesitated for a moment and then said, 'Sister—are you able to tell me what his condition is?'

The older woman said nothing for a moment and seemed to be looking Emma over—summing up whether she was sensible enough to be trusted with medical information. Then she seemed to make up her mind. 'So far, he has made slightly better progress than is usual in such cases and I thought he seemed a little better for your visit. But, you will understand, I cannot give you any promises.' Her severe expression softened a little. 'You are fond of him, yés?'

'Oh, very fond,' Emma said warmly. 'I've loved him all my life. He's a wonderful man.'

'That is good, he will have the courage to recover, then. You are English, Señorita Fairley?' and as Emma nodded, 'You speak our language very well, it is a help.'

It was indeed a help, reflected Emma, as she made her way back to the main hall of the hospital. It gave her confidence to find herself a taxi and give the address of the Hotel Redonda to the cheery driver in the big straw hat.

She was just about to step inside when she saw, to her horrified surprise, that the taxi was already occupied by three men, hefty ruffians in clothes that were anything but clean, who were obviously delighted that she should join them. They slapped each other, grinning, with repeated exclamations that she didn't understand, and the largest of them, a very tough-looking customer with leather-brown skin and long, tangled black hair, leered at her, holding out a massive, grimy paw. '*Linda señorita*,' he gloated, pulling on her hand.

Emma, alarmed, tried to pull back, but he hung on to her. The other two men joined in, shouting against

each other and flashing their teeth under long mous-
taches, in what seemed to her a very threatening way.

'Let me go, I've changed my mind,' she tried to
shout over the din, but the largest man was too strong
for her and she found herself dragged in into the taxi,
almost on to his knees, much to the vocal delight of his
companions.

Emma was almost weeping now; pictures of kidnaps
floated through her fevered imagination, of herself
being borne away to some remote desert hideout, to
languish for months. In desperation she stuck her head
out of the taxi window, just as it was moving into the
middle of the traffic, and yelled, 'Help—I want to get
out!' In English. Her Spanish had deserted her at this
moment of trauma.

Abruptly the door was wrenched open and Trent's
voice, shouted above the rest of the din, barked, 'What
the bloody hell's going on here?' He said something in
Spanish to the man who was holding her, who immediately released his grasp. Trent's arm was round
Emma, painfully tight. 'Jump,' he ordered, as the taxi
came to a halt in the middle of a traffic jam.

She jumped into his arms and he steered her through
the mass of cars, which one and all retaliated by honk-
ing their horns madly, but somehow they made it to
the side of the wide boulevard.

Emma's head was spinning wildly as Trent pushed
her down on to a seat under a tree. He put an arm
round her and held her gently but firmly, saying
nothing, until she opened her eyes and blinked up at
him dazedly.

'Well,' he said in a conversational tone, 'and what
exactly were you supposed to be doing?'

She gulped and dabbed her eyes. 'They asked me at
the hospital to f-fetch some things for Joe and I was
going to his hotel to get them.' Suddenly she shivered
violently, although the sun, beating down on the grass,
was blisteringly hot. 'I—I don't know what happened.

This cab came along and it seemed to be a cruising taxi, so I stopped it and then—these men were all inside and—and they frightened me, rather.'

To her annoyance Trent laughed aloud, but not unkindly. 'Silly child! You're not in England now, you know, with one-taxi-one-passenger. That was a *pesero* you hailed. They cram in as many passengers as they can at one time and take them where they want to go— mostly along the big main routes. I don't suppose for a moment the men intended to frighten you, they were just being very vocal in their admiration.' He chuckled. 'Mexican men are like that; they appreciate a pretty girl and have no inhibitions about saying so. I'm sure you weren't in any danger from them.'

'I'll take your word for that,' she said doubtfully, looking up at him. The eyes that met hers were narrowed whimsically, his hair shone like ebony in the dappled sunshine under the tree. His lips were parted slightly, showing strong, well-cared-for teeth. 'Anyway, thank you for rescuing me,' she said in a small voice. 'I was very glad to see you.'

His eyes held hers. 'And that,' he said huskily, 'is the first time you've admitted it. We're making progress.'

For a long moment their eyes were locked. Emma was acutely aware of his arm around her shoulders, of the closeness of his body to hers on the wooden seat, of the smell of the cologne he used, mingled with the dried-up grass all around them. Suddenly she was oblivious to the noise and hustle of the traffic. She felt weak with longing to rest her head against the hardness of his chest, under its silky cream shirt. She wished he hadn't been so kind and understanding. If he had bawled her out for her admittedly foolish action in rushing off on her own in a huge, unfamiliar city, she could have gone on resenting and disliking him. But now——

He stood up and held out both his hands. 'Are you

fit yet? Because if you are, I think we should both go along to Joe's hotel. I expect he left all the papers and notes relating to your tour together, and I'd like to get my hands on them. I've arranged to meet Roy Royston for lunch. I think we may be on to something really good there, and I want to be completely genned up so that we can begin to talk business. There'll be time to go through everything with you before lunch, if we get a move on.'

He took her hands and Emma allowed him to pull her to her feet. The shakiness had gone and for some reason she felt a sudden surge of energy. 'You mean—you really want me to help you?'

'Well, of course,' he said. 'I can't do without you, can I? So I'm afraid, Emma, you're stuck with me, like it or not. That is, if you care about Fairley Brothers' revival.'

He tucked his arm comfortably through hers as they set off across the grass in the direction of the hospital. 'I've got a taxi waiting,' he told her. 'A real taxi, the kind you find at the hotels, not one of your black-and-white-*peseros*.' He grinned down at her. 'You'll only have one quarter of a blatantly admiring Mexican to put up with this time. Think you can bear it?'

Walking close beside him in the sunlight, with the roar and scream of the traffic around them, Emma forgot about Lisa, forgot about Juanita, forgot about everything but the man beside her, his devastating masculine attraction and her entirely feminine response to it.

She gave him a little upward smile under her tawny lashes. 'I'll try,' she said, and a thrill ran through her as he squeezed her arm tight, and drew her against him.

'Partners?' he said, and for the first time she felt that it was possible. If she could believe what he said—that his only interest in her was because she was in Uncle Edward's confidence and because she and Joe

had been working closely together—then she couldn't
refuse. She thought fleetingly of Lisa. Lisa would be
hurt and disappointed to learn that Emma had gone
back on her word and was actively working with Trent
Marston. But Lisa was married now; she had her own
life to make with Richard. What had happened between
her and Trent couldn't be allowed to put at risk the
survival of the family firm because of bad feeling between one of the family and its newest recruit and
probable saviour.

They had reached the hospital entrance again now,
and Trent led her to a salmon-coloured car that was
waiting in the taxi-rank. He opened the door for her
and gave the address of the Hotel Redonda to the
driver.

As they drove out of the wide gateway he turned to
Emma. 'Partners?' he said again.

She nodded, with a flash of her quirky little smile.
'Partners,' she said, with a sigh. 'As you say, I've got
to put up with you.'

'We've got a little time before Royston is due to arrive,'
said Trent, glancing at his watch as he spread the
papers from Joe's briefcase out on the low coffee table
beside the sofa in their hotel suite.

Emma said, 'I must change out of these clothes and
get into something cool and fresh before I can put my
mind to anything. I won't be long.'

'Okay, hurry up.' He settled himself on the sofa and
picked up the top sheaf of papers.

Emma retired to the bedroom, where Trent had
carried her case, and closed the door. At first the
manageress of the Hotel Redonda—a swarthy, hard-
faced woman with beady eyes and black hair scraped
up on top of her head—had looked suspiciously at
Emma when she explained what she had come for. But
when Trent stepped forward, drawing out his note-
case and turning one of his charismatic smiles on the

woman, there was no more delay, and after that all was sweetness and light.

As the taxi-driver piled the suitcases into the cab Trent looked up at the façade of the Hotel Redonda, at the shabby, cracking plaster, the broken gold lettering, the dusty windows. He said, 'You wouldn't really have been happy here on your own, would you?'

Emma followed his look. 'I'd have got by,' she said hardily.

'Well, you don't have to,' said Trent, his hand at her arm as they got into the taxi. 'A truce has been declared, and we're both fighting on the same side now, remember?'

She looked out of the window as the taxi began to move, and suddenly the sun penetrated the thin smoggy haze that seemed always to hover over the city, and everything was bathed in a clean, clear light—the little market stalls that cropped up at random on the wide pavements; the Indian women peddling handicrafts; the boy flashing white teeth and holding a huge bunch of coloured balloons that floated up against the pale blue sky; there was even an oldish man carrying a portable organ strapped to his back and grinding out an old-fashioned waltz tune.

Emma turned to Trent, her face alive with interest. 'What a fascinating city this is,' she said.

'A city of contrasts,' he said with a sort of warm pride in his voice. 'Not all that long ago—less than couple of hundred years—it was a small, beautiful town of palaces and churches and noble buildings all centred round the Zocalo—that's the central square where the Cathedral is, we passed it on our way earlier—and then it started to grow and grow, more or less haphazardly. So now it's a city of surprises. I love it,' he added, 'you never know what's round the next corner.'

Emma turned her head and looked at his dark, handsome face, his eyes glittering now with pleasure. Yes, she had thought, you *would* like it. Mexico City is like you—full of surprises. Confusing. Unexpected. Vital.

Now, as she pulled off the beige suit she had worn since she arrived and opened the suitcase that Trent had dumped on the bed, she kept remembering the colourful scene they had passed through and she was gripped by a pleasant sense of excitement. Provided that Joe's condition continued to improve, it would be fascinating to spend a little time in this city that was so different from any other city she had visited in her travels with Joe. And now that she and Trent had somehow managed to put their relationship firmly on the basis of a friendly business co-operation, she didn't have to worry about that, either. She hummed one of the waltz tunes the organ-grinder had been playing and took out a dress from her case—a cotton dress in spring green with a little swingy jacket. It was mercifully uncrushed, and when she had touched up her make-up and brushed her hair she looked at herself in the mirror with the kind of satisfaction usually reserved for the times she had been going out for the evening with a new boy-friend.

But this was very different. This was the new Emma Fairley, the young business-woman, representing her family firm, partnering the dynamic Trent Marston. Nothing at all to do with romance!

Trent got to his feet as she opened the bedroom door and his eyes passed over her with appreciation. 'My, my,' he smiled. 'Very taking—you look as crisp as a fresh lettuce leaf. Now, come along and put me in the pciture.'

He put a casual arm round her shoulder, leading her to the sofa where he had been sitting. When they reached it he seemed to be about to pull her down beside him. Then he gave a wry little grin and pushed her towards a chair on the other side of the table. 'If we're going to talk business,' he said, 'I think you'd better be at a safe distance. Looking as tempting as you do at present you do terrible things to my concentration.'

Emma could have returned the compliment truthfully, for her skin was tingling where his fingers had touched it. Instead, she sat down without looking at him and said coolly, 'Shall we go through the papers, then?'

There was a short silence and still she wouldn't meet his eyes. 'Don't you enjoy being told you're desirable, then?'

'In the right time and place—yes.' She shuffled through the pile of papers busily.

Another pause. Then, 'Later, perhaps?' he said with a smile in his voice.'

Emma did raise her eyes then. 'Look,' she said quite forcefully, 'you suggested a business partnership and I agreed. I didn't have a casual flirtation in mind.'

His smile disappeared and the expression in the eyes that met hers and held them made her shiver inside. 'Neither had I, Emma,' he said slowly, seriously. 'Believe me, neither had I.'

He shook his shoulders, almost as if he were shaking off something that troubled him, and picked up the top sheet from the pile of papers on the table. It was a list that she had typed out for Joe in Houston. 'I'm not quite clear about the specifications here—and here——' He pointed with a gold pencil.

Emma took the sheet and stared down at it, trying desperately to concentrate. Being Trent Marston's business partner was going to be full of pitfalls that she had to avoid. If only she could understand him— even partly! But he was like a book written in a foreign language that you were only vaguely familiar with. You read a sentence and thought you had grasped its meaning and then a couple of sentences on you realised that you'd been entirely wrong. That was the effect Trent Marston had on her. A maddening man!

But for the next hour he was all the top executive—

asking questions, making notes, sitting silent for minutes at a time, deep in thought. Finally he closed the order book, looking rather grim. 'It seems rather worse than I imagined.'

Emma nodded, biting her lip. 'I know. We didn't do much good on that tour.' She studied his face and learned precisely nothing. She said, 'Are you wondering if you've backed the wrong horse?' How would she feel if he decided it was too late to save the firm, and just walked out? The cold emptiness she felt was quite shocking. She hadn't realised until that moment quite how much the new prosperity he had promised meant to her. 'Are you thinking of pulling out?'

'Pulling out?' The amazement in his face reassured her. 'Good God, no, that's the last thing I'd do. I like a challenge. If things come too easily I lose interest.' His dark eyes rested on her lazily, as if he were memorising the contours of her face. 'Haven't you noticed, Emma?'

Her inside stirred in a way she was becoming familiar with and she turned her head quickly. She would *not* gave him the satisfaction of seeing just how easily he could disturb her.

The telephone buzzed and Trent reached for it. 'Royston's here,' he told her, a moment or two later. 'Shall we go down?' He grinned. 'You can practise your sales technique on him, I'm sure he'll appreciate it.'

Emma gave him a look that was supposed to be withering and swept out before him to the lift, the green organdie dress rustling softly against her slim legs, her dark gold hair bouncing defiantly on her neck

The meeting was a success from the start. Emma took to Roy Royston—a stocky, middle-aged man with keen eyes and prematurely white hair above a brown, clever face. His frank, open manner was a relief, after the puzzle that was Trent Marston.

It seemed, however, that Trent reserved his deviousness for her alone, for over lunch in one of the hotel's big restaurants, nobody could have been more straightforward and forthcoming.

When the social preliminaries were over it was a working lunch and all the talk was of the new electronic device that Uncle Edward had been working on and which was, apparently, almost ready to go into production.

Emma said very little, although Roy Royston now and again drew her into the conversation with little questions about the history of the firm and about Uncle Edward—questions which she could answer clearly and with undisguised warmth and assurance. But Trent made it clear that she had been away from home recently and hadn't had time to catch up yet on new developments (it amused her that he said it as if she was poised to become an electronics expert at any moment), so she was able to relax and watch the two men and listen to the cut and thrust of their conversation.

And as she watched Trent she found herself reluctantly comparing the way he operated—quietly confident and enthusiastic—with Joe's much more unobtrusive manner. Trent wasn't showy and flamboyant—quite the contrary—but he wore confidence like a second skin, and she could see that Royston, the older man, thought highly of his opinion. They were two of a kind, she thought, and quite outside her league.

After lunch, the talk continued over drinks and coffee until Royston took his leave to keep another appointment.

'Au revoir, Miss Fairley.' He took her hand in both his and beamed at her. 'It's been a privilege meeting you and I'll sure look forward to doing business with both of you. 'We'll meet up again, Trent, before you leave Mexico.'

Trent walked with him to the entrance to the lounge where they had taken coffee, and then came back and dropped into the seat next to Emma. 'That went well,' he said with satisfaction. 'It's a good start. I think he'll take the agency, and he supplies some of the largest companies in Mexico.' He turned and smiled at her. 'Well done, Emma.'

'I didn't do anything,' she said.

'You didn't have to. Just being there was enough for the present.'

'It wasn't enough for me,' she said rather crossly. 'If I'm to be involved with you in this new venture I'll have to learn something about it. Do you think I could—have I got the intelligence?'

He laughed aloud and covered her hands with his, giving them a hard squeeze. 'Oh, Emma, Emma, you undervalue yourself. Of course you could learn—you're not just a pretty face. We're not supposed to be scientists; we're the marketing team. Edward thinks up the ideas, and we make sure they're produced and that everyone knows about it.' His eyes were shining. 'I can teach you all I know myself in a few hours—we'll start tomorrow. We'll make a splendid team.' He tossed off the remainder of his drink. 'What's the joke?'

She was smiling to herself. 'I was just remembering what Joe said this morning, when I told him about you. He told me I was to keep a tight hold on the reins and make you toe the mark.'

'Joe sounds a perceptive sort of bloke and I think he had something there.' His gaze travelled slowly over her, lingering on the low neckline of her dress, where the pleated white collar plunged demurely to the shadowy cleft between her firm young breasts. 'But I must warn you,' he drawled, and there were little devils dancing in his eyes, 'that it may prove more difficult than Joe—or you—imagines, to make me toe the line.'

'Oh!' she gasped, the heat rising to her cheeks. 'You're deliberately misunderstanding. I wish you wouldn't—wouldn't——'

'Wouldn't what?' he enquired smoothly. 'Wouldn't

pay you the odd compliment? It's inevitable, Emma, business partners or not. I'm a man and you're a woman, and that's the way it is.'

'You're infuriating,' she snapped. 'I don't know what you're trying to do, but——'

'I'd have thought it was plain enough by this time,' he smiled, 'but if you require a statement of intent, then I'm trying to make you fall in love with me.'

'Well, you won't succeed,' she flung at him. 'I wouldn't fall for you if you were the last——'

'—the last man on earth?' he cut in. 'Not very original, Emma, for a quick mind such as yours! Now come along, let's end this sparring match, stimulating though it is. I suggest we take Joe's things along to the hospital and get an up-to-date report on him. After that we'll put a call through to Edward and give him all the news.'

'I was going to write,' she began. International telephone calls were expensive and she and Joe had been economising for so long that it was second nature to avoid them. But Trent Marston wouldn't know what the word economy meant.

'You can write later,' he told her, a trifle impatiently. 'Now, let's get along. When we've been to the hospital we'll take a look in at this Trades Exhibition that you planned to visit with Joe. After that I'll treat you to a slap-up dinner to celebrate our success with Royston. Oh, and by the way, bring a coat or a wrap of some sort with you. It can get chilly in the evenings in Mexico City. We're about a mile and a half high, did you know that?'

'No, I didn't know,' she said shortly. She was smarting a little from the way he seemed to think he could give her orders, and decide what they should do, without consulting her. And even here there was no consistency about him. Sometimes he treated her as a partner and an equal, and sometimes as if she were a difficult child, who had to be either humoured or disciplined and shown who was master.

The annoying thing was that his way was usually proved to be right. What remained of the afternoon passed without a hitch. At the hospital they were told that Joe's condition was satisfactory and that she could see him again tomorrow. Later, back at the hotel, Trent put through a call to Uncle Edward and she was able to reassure him that all was going well.

After that they went by Metro across the city to the large building where the Trades Exhibition was being held, and wandered among the hundreds of stands showing everything from cabinets containing nuts and bolts, to the most intricate of modern developments in technology.

Trent missed nothing. He asked questions and chatted to the exhibitors, and examined the displays on every stand with the close scrutiny of a biologist who has just come across some new form of life. He was still brimming over with curiosity and enthusiasm when Emma's feet were aching and she was longing to sit down with a long, cool drink.

At last she could bear it no longer. 'Don't they provide seats in this place?' she moaned. 'I shall flop on the floor at any moment!'

He turned to her immediately. 'You poor sweet,' he said, and his voice was not mocking or teasing or flirtatious. It was—incredibly—tender and concerned. 'I've worn you out. What would you like to do? Shall we go back to the hotel and you can have a rest and a shower before dinner?'

'Sounds lovely,' sighed Emma, bemused by his quick change of approach. Bemused—and weakened. She wanted to go on disliking him, but he was making it difficult. Tough and tender—the mixture was a dangerous one.

Back in the hotel suite he said, 'Have a good rest while I do some telephoning. Let me know when you feel up to going out to dinner.'

Emma took a shower, put on a light wrap and lay on the bed. She wasn't sleepy; on the contrary she felt wide awake. She could hear Trent's voice in the next room, although she couldn't hear the words. She wondered if he was talking to Juanita.

And what did it matter to her if he was? Why did it give her a sick feeling inside to think of him with other women? They had agreed that they were simply business partners. They were going to work together on the exciting project of getting Fairley Brothers back on its feet again—and into the big time, if she had learned anything about Trent Marston. Already she had a good idea that he was what they call a money wizard. Just as long as it was only money that he bewitched, she thought, trying to see the funny side of this unsettled, yearning feeling she had, just listening to his deep voice on the other side of the door.

Suddenly she felt restless and couldn't lie here any longer. She got up and dressed in one of the unpretentious little cocktail dresses she had worn when she and Joe dined together at one of their modestly-priced hotels. By the time she had done her face and her hair Trent seemed to have finished his telephoning, and she went into the next room to find him stretched out on the sofa, blowing wreaths of smoke from a small cigar up towards the ceiling.

'Ready?' He swung his legs round and stood up. 'You look very nice, Emma.' It was casually said, just a run-of-the-mill compliment, and he didn't come near her or touch her as they went out together to the lift. He would still be thinking of Juanita, of course.

'The famous Zona Rosa is only a few minutes' walk away,' Trent said as they came out into the cool of the evening. 'We can take our pick of restaurants there; I've heard there are about four hundred of 'em all in quite a small area, to say nothing of the bars and shops and boutiques. The Zona Rosa is the swinging side of Mexico City. What do you fancy to eat?'

They turned into a brightly-lit street with blazing shop windows and smoothly-running cars and an air of subtle excitement, and Emma said, 'Goodness, I don't know—I leave it to you.'

'Then we'll find a nice safe American-style steak and salad,' Trent said, inspecting the signs outside the restaurants as they passed by. 'I won't suggest you go in for the fiery stuff. Anyway, unless you know the right places to go it's not easy to find really superb Mexican cooking, the kind that Mexicans give the ultimate praise to when they say it makes you "suck your fingers."'

Emma gave a mock shudder. 'I can't take anything really hot,' she said, and Trent laughed. 'Some day,' he said, 'I intend to find out if Emma Fairley is really as cool as she pretends to be.'

He was fooling, of course, making the kind of remark that a man is supposed to make when he takes a girl out to dinner, but Emma felt an odd little tug deep down inside her that warned, 'Be careful.'

But as the evening wore on she found herself relaxing with Trent, feeling easy in his company for the very first time. They ate juicy steaks with crisp, colourful salads at a small, intimate restaurant, and Trent ordered a bubbly wine that tasted of flowers. Afterwards there was a mouthwatering creamy concoction of unfamiliar fruits, and *café con leche*, and as they sat back, comfortably replete, Emma forgot that the man beside her, so handsome and assured and—what was the word?—so debonair—was someone that she needed constantly to be on her guard with. She giggled at his wry remarks as if they were old friends who had known each other for years.

They went out into the street again, crowded now with strollers and window-shoppers, with beautiful people unloading into the restaurants from gleaming fabulous cars, with all the trappings of affluence and high living.

Trent stood looking around for a moment, his face serious. 'And yet,' he mused as they turned to walk back the short distance to their hotel, 'within a stone's-throw of all this there are squalid dwellings; poor people who would live a whole day on the food we left on the table. They come streaming into the cities when they can't earn a living on the land. All the big cities are bulging at the seams. They try to get into America, too. They wade across the Rio Grande, believe it or not, and most of them are discovered and turned back by the Texan Border Patrol. I've seen it happening—it's pathetic.'

Emma was silent, walking beside him, keeping in step. Was this the big-business tycoon who lived to make money, who took his women where he found them and tossed them aside when he was tired of them? She felt as if she hadn't known him at all.

'Mexico is a wonderful country,' he went on quietly, 'and with vast natural resources. Some day she'll solve her problems, but just now one feels oneself longing to help these poor people to get going, to earn their own livings, to stand on their own two feet, as the saying goes.'

Emma linked her arm with his. 'You like mending things that are not working properly, don't you?' she said.

She felt him give a little start of surprise and thought that he had forgotten all about her for the moment. Then he grinned down at her. 'Perceptive lady,' he said. 'You read me like a book.'

She shook her head. 'Never—not a single line. You're a book written in a foreign language.'

Back at the hotel they went up in the lift. Trent paused at the door of the suite, his key in the lock. 'Are you going to invite me in for a goodnight drink?'

Emma looked up into his eyes, and that was a mistake, for her stomach flipped over and her heart began to race at what she thought she saw there.

She took refuge in flippancy. 'It's your suite, not mine.'

He was standing very still, very close. She was terribly conscious of his hard, muscular man's body beneath the thin texture of his suit. 'By the way,' she gabbled, her voice two tones higher than usual, 'we haven't discussed who's paying for this luxury pad. It's way out of my price range.'

He turned the key and held the door open for her. 'It's on the firm,' he said.

He closed the door behind them. Inside, the lights were dim, the big, luxurious room smelled faintly of cigar smoke, the air-conditioning hummed very softly, like a sleepy cat.

'Let me take your coat,' Trent said, and his voice sounded strained. Emma felt his hands resting on her shoulders, and the touch of them burned all through her. Her knees were trembling. She wanted to move across the room, to laugh and say something casual and ordinary, but she couldn't move.

Trent tossed her coat over the back of a chair. He, too, seemed reluctant to move.

They looked at each other in the shaded room. Then he said, 'Emma?' in a husky voice, and held out his arms.

Like a girl in a trance, she went straight into them.

CHAPTER SEVEN

IT was no calculated attempt at a seduction. It was an immediate, driving need for them both. Trent crushed her against him as if he were a drowning man clinging to someone who could save his life. Emma gasped for breath as she was pressed against the hard, muscular length of his body.

'Oh, Emma, my darling girl, you're so lovely—so tempting. I want you—every little bit of you——' His voice was muffled against her hair and his breath came warm and quick on her cheek. She was drowning too, and helpless to resist, as a drugged sweetness crept through her senses.

Her head tilted back as his mouth came down on hers in a long, exciting kiss, and her lips parted hungrily to his. She had never been kissed like this before, but it seemed the most natural thing in the world to wind her arms tightly round his neck, her fingers digging convulsively into the hair there, crisp and resilient to her touch. She felt warm, yielding, deliciously lost in the sensations he was arousing in her as his hands moved down her body, and she knew that she had been waiting for this ever since he kissed her that night of the wedding. Waiting and longing for it, even while she told herself she was hating him.

She gave a little moan as he picked her up easily in his arms and carried her to the sofa. For a heart-stopping moment she felt his weight on her, then he rolled away and knelt on the carpet, his face close to hers.

'I don't think,' he said in an odd, strangled voice, 'that I can stay here any longer unless you let me make love to you.' His eyes were burning into hers, the lids lowered, heavy. 'Will you, Emma?'

She lifted herself on to one elbow and stared dazedly at him, shocked into a sudden realisation of what she was doing. If Trent had said nothing, if he had taken her then and there, she knew she would have given herself to him without thought, in a white-hot turmoil of pure feeling.

But he had spoken and the spell was broken. He had given her a choice, and instinctively she drew back from the brink, her lips quivering.

'No,' she gasped, 'we must be mad! This isn't really what we want. It's just the wine and the s-surround-ings.' She looked vaguely round the intimately-lit, softly-cushioned room. 'No, Trent,' she said, and she realised with a small shock that it was the first time she had spoken his name. 'Don't let's spoil everything.'

He got slowly to his feet and she could see his body trembling and knew how hard he was struggling for control. '*Would* it spoil everything?' he said.

'Oh yes, of course it would.' She sat up, pulling her dress straight with shaking hands. 'You know it would. Partners, we agreed. Business partners.'

'That doesn't rule out any other sort of partnership as well.' He moved to take her in his arms again, but she drew away. 'Of *course* it does, don't you see?'

It would complicate everything. Not for him per-haps—it would mean very little to him. But she knew now that this man had the power to shake her world into fragments if she once let him love her. He would be an obsession with her, just as he had been with Lisa. And not for the world would she let a man like Trent—a man who had behaved so heartlessly once and would no doubt do so again if it suited him—not for the world would she let such a man come between herself and Lisa and spoil a lifetime of trust and affec-tion.

He was staring down at her almost angrily now. 'No,' he said roughly. 'I *don't* see. I believe you want it just as much as I do.'

Emma gave a little shrug. The memory of what he had done to Lisa had acted like a douche of icy water on her. 'Possibly,' she agreed in a small, controlled voice. 'You're a very attractive man, as you well know. We both got carried away, but we can see that it doesn't happen again.'

He frowned down on her. 'Is that really what you want, Emma?'

'Yes,' she said, almost serenely. 'That's what I want. We can get on very well as business partners, I think we've proved that to-day. Let's leave it that way.'

For a long moment Trent stood quite still. Then he shrugged and walked across the room to pour himself a drink. He tossed it off with his back to her, then he half-turned, not looking at her, and said coldly, 'Right. If I'm not wanted here I'll take myself off. We'll meet again in the morning, Emma, when we can resume our *business* partnership.' His lips curled into a sneer and the friendliness that had seemed to be growing between them all day had disappeared. He was bitterly, coldly angry, she could see that. It was probably better that way, she told herself bleakly. If he hated her for rejecting him then she might be able to throw off the subtle spell he had been casting on her. He wasn't a man who would take kindly to being refused.

He walked to the door. 'Goodnight, Emma, I'll remove myself from your presence.'

The irony in his voice stung her and the words seemed to speak themselves. 'To Juanita?' she heard herself say, in a high voice that she hardly recognised.

'Who else should I go to?' he said quietly, and went out and closed the door.

Trent was back next morning before Emma had finished dressing. He tapped at the bedroom door, calling out cheerfully, 'Good morning, Emma, ready for breakfast?' just as if they had parted last night on the friendliest terms. She sat before the dressing-table mirror, trying to cover up the ravages of another almost sleepless night, and felt like screaming 'Go away' at him. Instead, she managed to compose her voice and replied, 'I won't be long. Five minutes.' He had evidently decided to take her at her word and keep their relationship on a strictly business footing. Well, that was what she wanted, wasn't it? But there were so many questions that remained to be answered. For one thing she couldn't go on living in this luxury hotel, allowing him to pay the bill, even if he said it was 'on the firm'. Fairley Brothers simply couldn't rise to this sort of hotel and Trent Marston hadn't yet got complete control of the firm, so that he and nobody else could call the tune.

On the other hand she couldn't possibly leave Mexico until Joe was well and truly on the mend. She had come here to stay near Joe and that was what she was going to do. So—she and Mr Trent Marston must have a talk and get things sorted out, she resolved, plastering on far too much eyeshadow and removing it inexpertly with a tissue soaked in lotion.

She glared at herself in the mirror. 'You look a wreck,' she told herself, wondering when she was going to get a good night's sleep. Last night, after Trent had left, had been a disaster. She had sat for ages in front of a blood-and-thunder film on the TV, not taking in any of it, trying to forget the scene that had just taken place between Trent and herself. Trying not to think of him with Juanita; trying to pretend she didn't care. When, finally, she had gone to bed it was to lie sleepless for hours, wallowing in a confusion of thoughts and feelings that horrified and disturbed her.

'Five minutes up,' came Trent's voice cheerfully 'I'm coming in.'

The door opened and he appeared, looking as well-groomed and pleased with himself as he had looked the previous morning. If he and Juanita had spent a riotous night, Emma thought sourly, then he showed remarkably little evidence of it.

Emma was wearing a little green suit this morning, one that had stood her in good stead on her travels with Joe. It had white revers and a short, swingy top, and she had always felt pleasantly like a brisk young business woman in it. She didn't feel in the least brisk this morning, but Trent looked her over approvingly as he stood leaning against the doorpost. '*Very* nice,' he grinned. 'Most appropriate. I approve of my new business partner's taste in dress.'

'Thank you,' she said coolly, getting to her feet with a sidelong glance in the mirror to check on her eye-shadow.

As they went out to the lift Trent said, 'When we've had breakfast I'd like you to come back up here, if you will, please, and pack your things. I think it's time we moved on.'

She flicked a suspicious glance at him as the lift sucked them downwards. 'Move on? Where to?'

He raised dark brows. 'I'm not thinking of abducting you, if that's what's worrying you. I can take a firm "No" from a girl as gracefully as the next man, I hope.'

'Oh, I'm sure you can,' she said airily. 'I expect you have a long list of names in your little book, lined up in reserve.'

He burst out laughing, swinging the lift gates closed as they reached the ground floor. 'Does that bother you? You wouldn't by any chance be jealous?'

'Jealous? Of you? You're joking, of course.'

'No, I suppose you wouldn't,' he murmured thoughtfully as they walked across the thick carpet to the snack-bar where they had breakfasted yesterday. 'One is only jealous when one is in love—or so they tell me. Now I,' he continued conversationally, pulling out one of the red leather chairs for her, 'could be very, very jealous of you, Emma. So you can draw your own conclusions.' He pushed the chair in again with a little jerk as she sat down. 'What do you fancy for breakfast this morning? Coffee and rolls again? Or something more substantial?'

The abrupt change of subject told her that he was out to tease and bait her this morning, and the awful thing was that she had no defence ready. She hadn't expected him to behave like this after what had happened last night. She had thought he would be distant and cold. She supposed it was all part of this maddening man's technique. He took a malicious delight in surprising people.

'Just coffee and rolls, please,' she said. 'And I'd like my coffee black.'

He gave her a mocking smile as he turned away to the counter. 'Did madam have a bad night, then?'

The coffee was a life-saver. After the first few sips of the rich, dark, aromatic-smelling liquid Emma felt almost herself again, and ready to cope. 'You haven't told me where you propose to take me to,' she said.

'To my grandmother's home, up in Las Lomas, the hills beyond Chapultepec. My grandmother is looking forward to meeting you and she'll be delighted to put you up so that you can have a base here, and visit the hospital easily and frequently, as I'm sure you want to. For myself, I'll have to return to England in a day or two and I wouldn't like the idea of you staying alone in a hotel, Emma. I'm sure your uncle wouldn't, either.'

'I should be——' she began. She wanted to tell him that she resented being packaged and moved around and having her mind made up for her, but it would have seemed childish and petulant if he really were concerned for her well-being and safety. It was the kind of thoughtfulness she would have recognised in Joe, but she had to admit that it was a surprise to find it in Trent Marston.

He was watching her face closely. 'Please don't refuse, Emma. My grandmother really would like to meet you. At all events, we'll go up to her house after we've called at the hospital, and then you can see how the two of you get along. Agreed?'

He really was being provokingly thoughtful. 'Thank you,' she said, and added politely, 'It's very kind of your grandmother.'

'Oh, she *is* kind, and very easy to get along with. Not like her grandson. I'm sure you'll find her a pleasant change after a few days in my company.' His mouth twisted ironically and there was a slight, challenging twinkle in his black eyes, which Emma chose to ignore as she managed to choke down, with difficulty, the remainder of her roll. Sharing a meal with Trent Marston was a hazardous occupation.

At the hospital, later that morning, it was wonderful to find Joe so much better. 'I'll be back on the job in no time at all,' he declared. 'Meanwhile, how about bringing this young fellow who's filling the gap to have a heart-to-heart with me? I'd like to meet him.'

Emma's own heart sank. Trent was going to be a surprise to Joe, and not altogether a pleasant one. And it was her fault; she had deliberately misled Joe, she knew that. She just couldn't confront Joe with Trent Marston, the man who was all set up to take his job over—worse than that, to establish himself as Joe's boss, if she knew anything about Trent.

She stalled. 'Of course I'll bring him along,' she said, 'as soon as they tell me here you're fit to talk business. No, Joe dear, you're definitely *not* ready yet.' She squeezed his hand reassuringly. 'Very soon, I promise.'

She stayed a little longer today, arranging the flowers that she and Trent had bought on the way, telling Joe about the Trade Fair she had visited yesterday and about the meeting with Roy Royston. 'We met him at the Exhibition,' she said, prevaricating a little. 'Mr Marston happened to know him and he may be quite useful to us.' She talked on a little longer in an optimistic vein and finally left Joe looking quite cheerful, promising to come back again next day.

Trent was waiting in the corridor when she came out of the ward. 'This time,' he said darkly, 'I'm not risking you diving into a taxi to escape from me.'

'I wasn't——' she began, but he cut short her half-hearted protest with a disbelieving chuckle.

'Don't give me that, Emma, you know darned well you were. You've been trying to escape from me since the first moment you saw me—in the porch of the church in Dorset. And quite soon you're going to have to admit it. Also,' he added smoothly, as they came into the sunshine outside the hospital doors, 'you're going to have to admit that you can't escape from me—not ever.'

Emma gasped. The sublime conceit of the man! It stood out a mile, even when he was fooling.

But once again he gave her no chance to make a come-back, if indeed she could have thought of one. He said, 'We travel in style this time. I phoned my grandmother while you were with Joe, and she's sending her car to collect us. Ah, here it is now.'

An enormous, oldish black limousine, driven by a smiling Mexican in a flapping checked shirt and a shady straw hat, was pulling up outside the hospital entrance. He jumped out and threw open the car door and his grin became even wider as Trent thumped him on the shoulder in the friendliest way, saying, '*Hola*, Conrado, *cómo está usted?*'

The big Mexican gabbled away in Spanish, to which Trent listened, nodding and putting in a question now and again. It was, Emma gathered, all about Conrado's family, of which there seemed to be a very large number. Eventually Trent took her hand and drew her forward. 'This is Conrado, Emma, a very good friend of mine. Señorita Fairley speaks Spanish, Conrado,' he added, 'so you'd better watch what you say in her presence.'

Conrado roared with laughter and shook Emma's hand and they all piled into the big car, Emma travelling in the front seat between the two men. It was difficult, in the circumstances, for her to remain remote and dignified and she was urgently conscious of Trent's thigh pressing against hers, but to move away would only have confirmed his conceited boast that he had power over her, so she turned her attention to Conrado, smiling at his remarks, most of which were about a character called Matilde, who seemed to be attached to the household of Trent's grandmother in some unspecified way, and whose cooking drew forth the utmost scorn from Conrado. Matilde's *tacos de pollo* were, according to Conrado, only fit to be thrown to the pigs. He made a guttural noise in this throat and raised his eyes to heaven, narrowly missing hitting a boy on a cicycle.

Trent said sharply. 'Watch it, *amigo*,' and the Mexican looked sheepish and muttered, '*Lo siento*, Señor Trent,' and after that was silent.

Trent leaned his head to Emma's, waving a hand towards the passing scene as the car drove through a vast area of beautiful woodland. 'This is our famous Chapultepec Park,' he told her, 'of which we are justly proud.'

The road passed close to magnificent buildings, standing in green glades, with some of the most glorious trees Emma had ever seen. Far in the distance she glimpsed a lake, with islands and fountains, and there were fascinating paths leading mysteriously away into thickly wooded copses.

'What a heavenly spot,' she said, smiling spontaneously at Trent, forgetting to be on the defensive.

He grinned. 'There's a zoo as well,' he said, and that sounded so ridiculous that they both began to laugh.

Presently the road began to wind upwards into the hills, and eventually Conrado steered the car between high gateposts, topped with fabulous stone animals, and up a winding drive between bushes starred with yellow flowers.

When finally they pulled up at the house and got out of the car Emma stood lost in pure delight. 'This is simply lovely!' she breathed. 'I've never seen anything so beautiful.'

The house was obviously a copy of an American ranch-style dwelling long and low and white, with rows of windows catching the sunlight, and seeming to wink a welcome. Most of the houses—or rather, residences—that Emma had glimpsed on their drive through the wooded hills had been enormous, some of them even looking like Colonial-style mansions, and she had expected this one to be the same: rather intimidating. But it was nothing of the sort, it was a friendly house.

And the tall, white-haired woman who came from somewhere behind the house when she heard the car looked friendly too, in her blue cotton dress with a gardening apron tied round her.

She didn't wait for introductions. She pulled off her gardening gloves and took Emma's hands in hers. 'You're Emma Fairley and you're very welcome. Trent has told me a lot about you.' She looked over to her grandson, smiling fondly, and Emma could see the likeness between them: the same thin, intelligent face with its good bone structure; the same keen, observant glance; the same air of—what was it?—breeding perhaps.

She felt at home with this attractive elderly woman straight away. 'Thank you, *señora*,' she smiled. 'I hope he hasn't told you anything too bad about me.'

'All good, my child, all very complimentary.' The dark eyes in the wrinkled, sunburned face twinkled, and she looked more like Trent than ever—Trent when he was in one of his teasing moods.

She led the way towards the house, talking energetically in her warm southern drawl, enquiring after

Joe's progress, asking if they would like to have lunch straight away, or later. 'And you mustn't call me "*señora*", please, Emma. You must call me Juanita—everyone around here does.'

Emma caught her breath, stumbled, and would have fallen if Trent hadn't grabbed her arm to steady her. She couldn't take it in at once.

This was Juanita!—Trent's *grandmother*! Her brain spun wildly. He had known very well what she had thought, and he deliberately had not enlightened her. She threw him a glance of pure, smouldering resentment and shook off his restraining hand.

'Okay?' he enquired softly mocking. She drew in a hissing breath and drew quickly away from him, saying nothing. She was so angry that she wasn't capable of taking in much of the inside of the house, as they entered by way of a wooden veranda and a long window. She was only conscious of an atmosphere of comfort and space and light.

'May we have lunch straight away, please, Juanita?' Trent said. 'If it won't put Matilde out, that is. Is she in a good mood this morning?'

'Excellent,' smiled his grandmother. 'She's wildly curious to see Emma, though she wouldn't admit it for the world.' She took Emma's arm. 'Now, come along, my dear, I'll show you your room. Conrado will bring your bag.'

She led Emma along several passages and up a short flight of stairs. 'This is a winding sort of house,' she smiled over her shoulder, 'but you'll soon find your way around. Now, this is your room, I do hope you'll like it. Put Miss Fairley's case here, please, Conrado,' as the big Mexican appeared with Emma's case.

When he had departed Trent's grandmother put her hand on Emma's shoulder. 'I'm so very glad to have you with me, Emma, and I do hope you'll be happy here.' Her voice was warm and her eyes were kind.

Emma felt her own eyes prick with tears. After all

that had happened in the last few days she felt she had found sanctuary in this lovely house. 'I'm sure I shall, and thank you so much,' she said quietly.

The elderly woman moved towards the door. 'I'll leave you to settle in, then,' she said. 'Come down when you're ready and we'll have lunch. Trent seems to be in a hurry to eat—I seem to remember he said he has an appointment this afternoon, so perhaps we can get rid of him and then you and I can have a lovely talk and get to know each other.'

She remained standing beside the door, her eyes fixed on Emma's face. 'I can see why Trent is so attracted to you, Emma. You're a little like his mother, she has the same dark gold hair and funny little smile.' She nodded, went out, and closed the door gently behind her.

Emma sank down on the soft bed. So Trent had told his grandmother he was attracted to her, had he? And why, exactly, had he done that? She passed a hand wearily across her forehead. She would have to give up trying to guess the man's motives; they were completely unfathomable. Perhaps Juanita (she must get used to calling her that, although it seemed strange at first) perhaps Juanita could throw some light on the way her grandson's cryptic mind worked.

Emma sighed as she stood up and began to explore the large, pleasant bedroom with its adjoining small bathroom, trying to concentrate on what she was looking at, but she scarcely took it in at all, for her thoughts were churning round and round, centred on Trent. She didn't seem to be able to get him out of her mind, and yet she had reached a state of complete bewilderment where he was concerned.

There was a fascination about mystery. Was that why he filled her thoughts constantly? Why seeing him afresh gave her a curious little lurch in the pit of her stomach? Why her pulses beat wildly when he touched her?

She hoped fervently that it was merely the attraction of the unknown that was playing such havoc with her usually calm disposition. It would be appalling if she found out that she had fallen in love with the man.

She sat down at the dressing table and began to tidy her hair and check on her make-up. Whatever the answer to the riddle, it would be easier now that she was here in his grandmother's house and she wouldn't be alone with him all the time.

Juanita—Trent's grandmother! How absurd that mistake had been! But the smile that she saw reflected in the mirror wasn't one of amusement. With a kind of horror she decided that she looked quite disgustingly smug.

As Emma had hoped, everything became much easier from then on. Trent had arranged to fly back to England in two days' time, and Emma would stay on with Juanita and keep in close touch with Joe's progress. Juanita—bless her—insisted that Joe should come back to her home in the hills when he was released from hospital. The length of his stay could be decided later.

'Your grandmother is incredibly kind,' Emma said to Trent as he was driving her to the hospital on the day before he was due to leave. 'I really don't know why she should do all this for Joe and me.'

'Don't you know—*really*?' As he stopped the car outside the hospital Trent sat sideways in his seat and turned his gaze full on her. 'Juanita likes you very much, but more than that, I'm her one and only grandson and you're my girl.'

'I'm not—how could you tell her that?' Emma spluttered indignantly.

He patted her hand as if she were a fractious child. 'Let's call it wishful thinking, shall we?' he grinned, and got out of the car. 'And as for Joe,' he added as they passed through the big doors of the hospital, 'Joe

is a valued member of our firm, so of course Juanita
would want to help.'

To-day Trent asked to see the doctor who was looking after Joe's case. 'Señor Kent is getting on very well
indeed,' the young doctor told them. 'If there are no
setbacks he should be allowed out of hospital in ten to
fourteen days. Then he must rest and take it easy for
at least two months. Can that be arranged? It would
not be safe for him to travel back to England.'

Emma left them talking and went in to see Joe.
'You're looking heaps better,' she told him, sitting
down by the bed and squeezing his hand hard. 'And I
see you've heard from Uncle Edward.' She indicated
an envelope addressed in Uncle Edward's handwriting,
which was lying on the locker. How much had Uncle
Edward told Joe about Trent? she wondered nervously.
Tact wasn't her uncle's strong point; he lived in a
world of his own and wasn't always conscious of other
people's reactions and feelings, although basically he
was a very kind man.

Joe said, 'Read it yourself, love,' and she reached for
the envelope.

Uncle Edward had been the soul of tact this time.
He had sent a get-well card (purchased, no doubt, by
Jessie at his request) with a picture of a white-sailed
yacht ploughing through rough blue water. Inside he
had written: 'Let go of the wheel for a while, old boy,
until you're really fit again. We'll put her on automatic
steering and ride out the storm. Regards always,
Edward.'

Emma replaced the card on the locker, and Joe
grinned his old wry grin and said, 'Must obey the captain, mustn't we?' He leaned his head back against the
pillow, looking suddenly more tired. 'Is this bloke
Marston with you now? If he is I'd like to take a look
at him. Just for a couple of minutes.'

Emma said anxiously, 'Will they let you have more
visitors?' If he didn't take to Trent—if he suspected

that Trent was a climber who was out to insinuate himself into Joe's own place in the firm—if he got upset and worried, she didn't dare think what that might do to his chances of making a good recovery.

Joe saw her hesitation. 'Please, love,' he begged.

In the corridor Emma found Trent now engaged in conversation with the stern-looking Sister, who wasn't looking at all stern at the moment.

Emma plunged in with, 'Sister, may Mr Kent have another visitor? I think he may be worrying about his work and as Mr Marston is taking over his job for the moment it might be helpful if they could meet.'

The Sister beamed at Trent. '*Si, si,* you may go in for just a few minutes, Señor Marston. You will make his mind easy, I am sure.' She straightened her already immaculate apron and swished away down the corridor.

Emma looked after her, compressing her lips. Another conquest for Mr Trent Marston! He bowled them over like ninepins. 'You'd better come in, then,' she said coolly.

He must have heard the reserve in her voice. He put a hand at her elbow as they went into the small ward, and gave her arm a reassuring squeeze. 'Trust me, Emma, just this once,' he whispered. 'I promise I won't say anything to upset him.'

She moved away from him as they approached the bed. She didn't want Joe to get any wrong ideas about her relationship with Trent Marston. She wanted him to make up his own mind about the man who was stepping into his job.

'You'd better not,' she returned fiercely under her breath.

She needn't have worried. From the first moment she could see that the two men liked each other. She knew Joe so well, had watched him with other men, and respected his opinions about them. It shook her that he so obviously accepted Trent immediately as a man to be trusted. She didn't know whether to be pleased or not.

They stayed only a short time before the Sister appeared at the door. Trent got to his feet. 'Time's up, it seems.' He stood looking down at the man in the bed regretfully. 'There's a whole heap of stuff I'd like to talk over with you and ask your advice about, Joe, but it will have to wait until you're fit again. Meanwhile, will you trust me to do the best I can—with Emma's help?'

Joe's tired blue eyes moved to Emma and back to Trent. 'Oh yes,' he said simply. 'I'll be happy to leave everything to the two of you.' He smiled faintly. 'I can see you'll work well together.'

Emma bent over the bed and kissed him, hiding the tears that pricked behind her eyes. She knew how much Joe had valued their partnership, but now he was handing her over without a scrap of resentment.

As the door of the ward closed behind them she murmured chokily, 'He's rather wonderful, isn't he?'

Trent linked his arm with hers. 'He's a good fellow,' he agreed. 'I hope he'll make a quick recovery and be able to get back on the job. The firm will miss him.'

Lunch was set out on the veranda overlooking the garden when they got back to the house on the hills. 'Señora Juanita has lunched already,' Matilde told them, speaking in her quick, excited Spanish. 'She has gone to have a rest and says she will see you both later.'

Matilde was a gaunt, grey-haired woman with a face criss-crossed with wrinkles. She eyed Emma and Trent with avid interest out of beady black eyes as she served their lunch of chicken rolled up in tortillas and fried crisply, with tomatoes and beans and shredded lettuce, followed by an enormous dish of colourful, exotic fruits and little biscuity cakes.

'I can't think why Conrado complains of Matilde's

cooking,' Emma said, after Matilde had served their coffee and left them. 'That was a gorgeous meal.' She spoke in a high, rather jerky tone, for in fact she was feeling the old tension gripping now that she was alone in the house with Trent for the first time since they arrived here.

He leaned back in his wicker chair, eyeing her with pleasure as she sipped her coffee. The veranda was shaded by a huge tree and Emma's creamy skin and the soft folds of the delphinium-blue dress she was wearing were dappled with little shadows.

'Gorgeous,' echoed Trent lazily, his eyes moving over her.

Something in his voice made her heart begin to thump. 'I suppose you'll be leaving early in the morning?' she said, not looking at him.

'I'm leaving today, as a matter of fact,' he said. 'I'm dining with friends who live quite near to the airport and they're giving me a bed for the night.'

'Oh,' said Emma, surprised at the quick feeling of disappointment she felt. She should have been relieved that Trent was leaving, but suddenly the weeks ahead seemed to stretch rather emptily. It could be, she told herself hastily, that she was going to miss the challenge he presented, rather than the man himself.

A quizzical smile touched his mouth. 'They really are just friends,' he said, eyeing her with amusement. 'A married couple, in fact, so you needn't be suspicious this time.'

'I don't know what you're talking about,' she told him coldly.

'I think you do. When I left you at the hotel you had all sorts of nasty thoughts about some girl-friend I was going to spend the night with. And all the time it was simply Juanita.'

She glared at him. 'You meant me to think that, didn't you?' she accused. 'You just wanted to make a fool of me.'

Trent shook his head, smiling. 'Not a bit of it. I wanted to see how you'd react—if it mattered at all to you. And it did, didn't it, Emma? Go on, admit it.' He leaned across the table and put his hand over hers.

'Oh,' she burst out in exasperation, dragging her hand from under his, 'you really are the—most—impossible—man! I never know whether to believe you—whether you're serious or not.'

She couldn't sit here any longer continuing this absurd conversation. She put down her coffee cup with a little clatter and stood up, walking away from him down the garden.

He came after her, of course. 'It's a pleasant afternoon for a walk,' he said smoothly. 'Suppose I show you the glories of Juanita's garden? I don't think you've seen all of it yet.'

So far, Emma had not gone beyond the terraces, and the exotic shrubs that rioted in the flower beds and spilled over on to the lawns. But now Trent put a hand at her elbow and urged her forward to a wilder part of the garden, under the dense foliage of overhanging trees that turned everything into a blue-green shade. It was cool here, and she could just hear the splash and trickle of water somewhere near.

They came out into a small clearing and before them the land fell steeply away in a tumble of rocks, ending in a narrow gorge some ten feet below. A stream cascaded down between the rocks, sending up fountains of spray that glistened in rainbow colours where the sunlight pierced the shade of the trees.

There was a wooden safety rail at the edge of the rocky decline, and Emma leaned on this, looking down to where plants and ferns sprung from between the wet, mossy rocks, and small, brightly-coloured birds fluttered and clung, pecking at unseen insects.

'It's beautiful,' she breathed, forgetting everything else in her pleasure. 'Like fairyland. You expect to see Oberon appearing through the trees.'

Trent laughed. 'You can have your fairy king. I prefer the fairy queen myself.'

She was glad he was keeping everything light. It would be so much easier to part on a note of friendship and nothing more. But even as the thought occurred to her, a silence fell between them and she could think of nothing to say. She was desperately conscious of his tall, hard body close to hers and she wanted to move away, but some stronger spell kept her motionless.

She swallowed and her throat was dry, and the silence went on and on until she could bear it no longer. She half-turned, to look up at Trent, and what she saw in his face made time stand still. Then, very slowly, he reached out and stroked back her hair, cupping her face between his hands, looking down at her with a tenderness she wouldn't have believed him capable of only an hour ago.

'Emma?' he breathed. The word was a question, and like a girl in a dream she moved towards him and went into his arms.

The moment had a kind of inevitability, and she knew hazily that everything that had happened since the first moment they looked at each other had been leading up to this. His mouth came down to hers and she gave herself up to his kiss, to the fondling of his hands, with a hunger that held a primitive desperation. They clung together, their bodies moving against each other, a man and a woman sharing a mutual need and fierce pleasure.

His mouth buried itself in the softness of her neck, trailing slowly downwards as she arched her body back, and finding the deep cleft between her breasts. Her arms went up and her fingers wound themselves in the crisp hair at the back of his neck, digging into the taut muscles there, and again their mouths met, probing and searching each other in a kind of frenzy, as if they could become one person instead of two.

Suddenly she heard Trent groan and he pulled himself away from her, his arms dropping heavily to his sides. His face was haggard and he was shaking all over. 'This isn't the way I planned it,' he said roughly. 'You see what you do to me, Emma.' It sounded like an accusation.

He moved away and stood with his back to her, struggling for control. She stood rigid, suddenly afraid of what he would say next, knowing at last that this was the man she wanted with a burning, clamouring need, in spite of all that had happened. Her love had grown secretly, like a seed growing in the dark, and now it had burst into flower and there was nothing she could do about it.

'Trent,' she whispered, longing for the feel of his arms around her again.

But when he turned back to her there was something in his face that frightened her. The tenderness had gone and the passion too, and all she could find there was his usual wry humour. 'It seems we do something to each other,' he said. 'Perhaps we should get back to the house, out of the way of temptation.'

She felt pain, as if he had struck a steel blade into her, but she managed to hold her head high and put an answering smile on her mouth. 'I think you're right,' she said, 'it would be a pity to complicate things, wouldn't it?'

Juanita had come downstairs and was sitting in her basket chair on the veranda, a gracious, elderly lady with her white hair beautifully coiffured and her long violet-blue dress hanging in soft folds around her chair. She greeted them happily, enquiring about the news of Joe from the hospital, and they sat and talked to her for a while before Trent got to his feet and announced that he must be leaving. 'Conrado's going to run me down into the city, if that's all right with you, Juanita.'

'Of course, my dear boy, I'm only sorry you're leaving us so soon. But glad you're leaving Emma behind to be company for me.' She gave Emma a warm, smiling glance.

There was a warning hoot from round the front of the house and Trent grinned. 'He'll never learn, will he?' He bent and kissed his grandmother. 'Goodbye for now, dear one, look after yourself,' and she held him close for a moment in a tight little hug.

Emma had a hollow feeling inside. Would he just say goodbye to her and walk away? But he paused in front of her chair, looking down at her. 'Coming to see me off?' he said steadily.

She got up and walked beside him down the steps of the veranda and along the path that skirted the side of the house. He didn't take her arm, or touch her. He simply said, 'Wish me luck, Emma. By the time we meet again maybe Fairley Brothers will have a new look. There's a lot to be done, but I'm looking forward to it.'

'Of course I wish you luck,' she told him rather woodenly. This was what she had asked for, wasn't it? To be his business partner and nothing more.

Conrado was sitting in the big black car. 'Your bag's in the back, Señor Trent,' he grinned cheerfully, leaning over to open the door.

Trent put a hand on the door. Then he bent and kissed Emma briefly on the cheek. 'Au revoir, Fairy Queen,' he smiled. 'We'll be in touch.'

He got into the seat beside Conrado, and the engine began to purr. Conrado pushed in the gear, but as the car moved forward Trent said quickly, 'Stop a minute, *amigo*.' He leant out of the open window. 'Just remember, Emma, that you've got me all wrong. You think I've been trying purposely to play the fool and mislead you. But the truth is that I've meant every word I've ever said to you. Cross my heart, my darling girl. Every single word. Think about that while we're apart. will you?'

Emma just stared at him, in stunned silence, her eyes

wide. He had surprised her many times, but this was the biggest shock of all.

He held her eyes for a moment longer, as if he couldn't bear to go, and then he turned briskly and said, 'OK., *amigo*, drive on.'

The big car purred away down the drive, and Trent looked back and lifted a hand in salute as it turned the corner out of sight.

Emma stood for a long time, looking at the place where it had disappeared. Then, very slowly, she walked back to where she had left Juanita, and there was a pink glow on her cheeks and a shine in her tawny eyes; so unmistakably a girl in love that Juanita's own dark eyes twinkled knowingly.

She patted the chair beside her. 'Come and sit down, my child,' she said in her soft southern drawl, 'and let's talk about my wonderful grandson.'

CHAPTER EIGHT

IN the days that followed there was a great deal of talk about Juanita's wonderful grandson—in fact, Trent was the principal topic of conversation between the two women, the old one and the young, who both loved him.

Juanita seemed to take it for granted that Emma would soon become one of the family, and Emma hadn't the heart to say that it was most unlikely. She assured herself of that frequently, not allowing herself to believe that Trent's remarks when he said goodbye were meant to be taken at their face value.

But when she was alone at night she dredged her memory and came up with the inescapable fact that he had said over and over again, in different ways, that he was in love with her. And what did that mean? A serious, permanent relationship, or merely a temporary affair—a convenient arrangement between business colleagues? She wished she knew.

His frequent telephone calls didn't make things any clearer. They were all about the business, his plans and hopes. He was reorganising the office and the workroom completely. 'You won't recognise it when you get back,' he told her. He was living at her home in the village. That suited both him and Edward splendidly. Edward didn't want to waste his time coming in to the office in Poole, and this way Trent could be in touch with him daily for conferences when he went back in the evening. 'Jessie's a brick,' Trent said. 'She's looking after me like a mother.'

Usually Uncle Edward came on the line finally, enquiring about her well-being and about Joe's progress. Lisa wasn't mentioned by either of them and Emma

163

couldn't bring herself to ask any questions. The thought of Lisa, and the way Trent had treated her, was like an old wound that hadn't healed. You could forget about it sometimes and then suddenly it began to hurt and niggle.

She promised herself that she would write to Lisa; then the letter would be waiting at Lisa's new home when she got back from her honeymoon at the end of the month. Surely, by then, Lisa wouldn't care too much that Emma had been in Mexico with Trent, and that even now was staying with his family there. But in case Lisa still felt some lingering bitterness, she would reassure her that her own involvement with Trent Marston had been purely a matter of business, and that it was because of Joe's illness that they had come to Mexico together. But the longer she put off writing the letter the more impossible it became to write it. Finally she bought a greeting card with a picture of the Floating Gardens of Xochimilco on it and wrote, 'I bet you haven't got anything like this in the Seychelles! My best love to you both. Have a super time and I'm longing to see you when we all get home again. Your Emma.'

She felt a faint sense of relief when she had posted the card. It would be so much easier to explain things to Lisa when they actually met. So she pushed the niggling doubt into the background again and began to enjoy her stay.

Each day she visited Joe in hospital—the talkative Conrado driving her there and back and amusing her with his frank comments on the way of the world, for which he hadn't anything very good to say. Señor Trent, however, could do no wrong, apparently. He was—Conrado rolled his eyes, searching for the most complimentary word—*caballeresco*, which Emma interpreted as meaning a very chivalrous gentleman. It wouldn't have fitted her own opinion of Trent only a short time ago. But now—she wasn't sure. She had seen a different side of him in Mexico.

And Juanita, with the adoring indulgence of a grandmother, was never tired of singing his praises. His strength, his kindness, his idealism, his generosity! It sounded to Emma much too good to be true, but she found herself lapping it all up eagerly, wanting to believe every word.

From Juanita she learned about Trent's parents. About his father, Juanita's only son, who owned a merchant bank and was at present working and living in Hong Kong with his English wife, Sylvia. Juanita seemed to approve of her daughter-in-law, who was, she kept on saying, quite remarkably like Emma herself. 'She'll love you too,' Juanita promised, 'I know she will.' Emma decided that that was a somewhat rash statement, but even that pleased her because it seemed to give her a stronger link with Trent.

'Robert and Sylvia would have liked Trent to follow his father into the bank,' Juanita said, 'but that was too dull a prospect for him. He needed the excitement of the business world. He loves a challenge.'

Emma heard how, in the ten years since he left Cambridge at twenty-three, Trent had saved no fewer than three ailing firms from bankruptcy, and put them on the road to recovery again.

'Trent's lame ducks, his father calls them,' Juanita laughed. 'I don't think Robert quite approves, it all seems a bit risky to him, as a banker, but Trent thrives on it.'

'And then, when he has saved the firms—what happens?' Emma asked. This was something she had to know.

'Oh, he moves on, looking for another lame duck,' his grandmother told her proudly. 'There's no holding Trent.'

No holding Trent! That about summed it up. There was a tight constriction in Emma's throat. One day, whatever happened between her and Trent, he would 'move on'. He wanted change, new challenges, he wasn't a man to settle down; the thought was infinitely depressing. For hours afterwards there was ice in her veins as she determined to conquer this painful yearning to see him, to be held close in his arms; then he would telephone again and just hearing his voice melted her resolution and the fever came hotly back.

Joe improved ever more rapidly as each day passed and Emma's visits to the hospital became longer. She told him everything that Trent had told her about the rebuilding of the firm's fortunes and about his plans and his contacts and Uncle Edward's new navigational instrument, which was soon to go into full production. Joe listened, and nodded, and was obviously delighted, and Emma felt that she should be delighted too, only this agonising doubt about the future gnawed away at her all the time.

Juanita insisted on Emma going out and seeing some of the sights of Mexico City. She herself wasn't up to the noise and bustle, she said regretfully, but there was an old friend of theirs, a delightful Mexican gentleman, now retired, who was at the house constantly, and who drove Emma on several sightseeing trips himself, and also arranged for her to join a couple of guided tours to places of interest.

She stood in awe below the colossal pyramids at San Juan de Teotihuacán while the guide explained that the Toltecs, who built them originally, nearly two thousand years before, had later considered the place cursed and deserted it; she visited the Cathedral, built on the site of the Great Temple of the Aztecs; she saw the modern famous new library at the University, where the walls were covered by mosaics made from natural stones from all over Mexico. The theme of the murals was Mexico's heritage—Aztec and Toltec, as well as tribute to the Spaniards for what they had done for the country. There was, she was told, space for over a million volumes.

She was taken to the Basilica of Nuestra Señora de Guadalupe, a shrine built on the spot where the Virgin is said to have appeared to an Indian in the sixteenth century; and the Castle of Chapultepec, which was once the residence of the Emperor Maximilian and the Empress Charlotte.

The tourist trail was interesting, Emma found, but most of all she enjoyed the afternoons she spent alone at the Museum of Anthropology, where the whole history of Mexico was displayed. Here she wandered for hours as she was transported back into ancient civilisations of which she knew nothing and had only vaguely heard about. But this was Trent's heritage, and that gave it all a fascination quite apart from the interest of the impressive exhibits themselves. When they met again, she planned, she would have so much to discuss with him, so many questions to ask. By the time Conrado picked her up at the prearranged time outside the Museum she felt quite intoxicated by all she had seen and experienced.

Then, at last, came the day that Joe was released from hospital. Juanita had already visited him once, with Emma, and had been able to give him her invitation in person. Now he arrived and was installed in a pleasant ground-floor room overlooking the gardens, and from then on life changed for Emma. She went out less, was content to stay around the house. Juanita suggested engaging a day-nurse, but Emma demurred, saying that she could surely do all that was required for Joe. And so she did, and found that everything worked out smoothly and happily. It was as if time were suspended as the hours passed, sitting in the beautiful garden, looking after Joe and seeing that he rested most of the time and took just the prescribed amount of exercise and didn't forget to take his tablets.

In May, the weather became warmer and decidedly wetter. Hardly a day passed without a shower. Juanita was jubilant as her beloved garden burst into a blaze of colour. In June, there was almost too much rain and many days were spent indoors. Emma's Spanish became fluent as she practised on everyone in sight, including Juanita's elderly friend Luis Valesco, with whom Joe had struck up a friendship. The two men talked for hours together, with Joe yarning about his days as a young man in the R.A.F. and Señor Valesco, in his painstaking English, recounting stories of the colourful history of his own country, that had seen so much change in his lifetime.

Then, at last, came the day for Joe's final check-up at the hospital. He came away beaming. 'All clear,' he told the waiting Emma. 'I can travel at any time. I have to see my own doctor as soon as I get home, but Dr. Martinez thinks there's no reason why I shouldn't start work again in a couple of weeks, if I take it very easy.'

And so, on a misty morning in early July, Joe and Emma said goodbye to Juanita, with gratitude they could hardly find words to express. 'Don't try, my dear Emma. I've loved having you—and Joe too.' Juanita kissed Emma and held her away, looking affectionately into her face. 'Just tell that grandson of mine to bring you back to see me very, very soon.'

Joe managed the long plane journey well, sleeping most of the time. Emma, on the other hand, was wide awake from the time of take-off. She found herself dreading the moment she would see Trent again. Her thoughts had gone round and round so often in the past weeks that she had almost begun to believe, by now, that she had dreamed those words he had spoken as he said goodbye on the day he left. Surely, if he had really been in love with her he would have followed it up, would at least have written to her, done more than merely put through the occasional telephone call, which was as much for Juanita as for her. All through the long flight her doubts became miseries and by the time they landed at Heathrow she had convinced herself that he couldn't possibly have been serious. When had she ever been able to believe what he said? Probably by now he had found himself another girl-friend—several girl-friends. She must be prepared for that. She wouldn't show him she had missed him and longed for him every moment since he left.

As they disembarked she tried to forget about Trent and concentrate on looking after Joe. When they finally came within sight of the arrivals lounge, with all the eager faces lining the long side barrier, she said, 'Keep a look-out for Malcolm. Uncle Edward said he would be sure to be here in good time.' Her eyes passed over the row of faces, searching for Malcolm's thick thatch of greying hair and craggy face. Finally, they came out into the main hall, but there was no sign of Malcolm. Emma stood uncertainly, looking around, hoping for Joe's sake that there wasn't going to be any hitch now, at the end of this long, tiring journey.

Then, coming towards her, she saw Trent, and felt a jolt in her stomach that was quite sickening. He had seen her now—she saw him give a start of recognition—and was pushing his way through the crowd towards her. At the same time she started to run towards him and they met with a head-on crash, and then she was in his arms and he was holding her tightly against him and kissing her, and all the uncertainty and questioning of the last weeks was over.

Joe came up, grinning. Trent wrung his hand without letting go of Emma. 'And how's Joe? You're looking fine. Gosh, it's great to see you both again, I've got so much to tell you.'

This was a different Trent, younger, laughing, almost boyish. Emma felt as if she were dissolving in love for him.

From then on he took charge of everything and half an hour later they were all in Trent's big car, with Joe settled comfortably at the back, nodding off to sleep again.

Trent pushed in the gear-lever. Then he turned to Emma and put a hand on her knee and said, very low, 'It's been a long wait, my darling, but we're going home now. And I've got a surprise for you.'

'That's nothing new,' she laughed, thrilling to the touch of his hand. 'You're always surprising me.'

'Wait till you see this one, though,' he said mysteriously. He let in the clutch and the car moved slowly out of the car park.

Not much more than two hours later they drew up at the door of the house by the sea. Jessie and Malcolm were out on the steps, in the gathering dusk, and even Uncle Edward had deserted his work-room for once to join the welcoming party. When the greetings were over Jessie bore Joe away to the room she had prepared for him; Malcolm took Trent's car to the garage; and Uncle Edward beamed on Trent and Emma, and invited them to his study 'for a celebratory drink'.

He knows, thought Emma. He knows and he's pleased. Oh, everything was coming beautifully right. In a haze of happiness her eyes met Trent's over the rim of her glass.

Later, she went up to her room to unpack. Trent came after her, carrying her travel bag. In her room he closed the door and held out his arms. They clung together as if they had been apart for years, and Emma felt her tears wet on Trent's hard cheek.

'It *is* true?' he said shakily at length. Somehow they had got on to the bed and she was sitting half-cradled in his arms. 'You will marry me?'

'Try to stop me,' she said, and he gave a long, long sigh and tightened his arms round her, his cheek against her hair.

'It was hell, leaving you behind in Mexico,' he said. 'I had to practically handcuff myself to the office desk to stop myself getting on the next plane back again

But I reckoned I had to give you time. I knew I'd got off on the wrong foot with you—that you thought I was an unfeeling bastard. You told me so, if you remember. So I had to leave you and hope you'd miss me as much as I missed you. Did you miss me, my love?'

'Every single minute,' she whispered, and turned into his arms again, her mouth seeking for his in a long ecstatic kiss.

From downstairs came the sound of Jessie pounding on the gong, announcing dinner. Trent lifted his head. 'Damn,' he muttered. 'Who wants food?'

Emma struggled out of his arms, straightening her dress. 'I do,' she grinned. 'I couldn't eat a thing on the plane. I was too scared at the thought of seeing you again and finding you didn't want me—that you hadn't meant what you said.'

He took both her hands and held them tightly. 'I'll never lie to you, Emma,' he said soberly. 'You do believe that now, don't you?'

'Yes,' she said slowly, looking deep into his eyes. 'Yes, I believe that.'

It wasn't until after dinner that Trent announced to Emma reluctantly that he had to catch the night train back to London. 'I've got an important meeting at nine tomorrow morning that I can't very well get out of, but I'll come straight back the very second it's over, I can promise you. Let's meet at the office at one, shall we? Then I can show you my surprise.'

Emma's Mini was back in the garage by now, resplendent in its new coat of white paint after its respray. She drove Trent to the station to catch his train.

'Only a few hours this time, my darling.' He kissed her hungrily as the train drew in to the platform. 'Love me?'

'Always.' She clung to his hand until the very last minute, and then stood watching as the train snaked out of the station, bearing him away from her.

As she walked slowly down the platform she told herself she was the luckiest girl in the world. It was quite ridiculous that she should feel suddenly as if a dark shadow had fallen across her happiness.

Back at home there was an unfamiliar white car parked at the front door. Who on earth had called at this time of night? One of Uncle Edward's scientist friends, probably. They had a habit of dropping in on him at all sorts of unreasonable hours.

The hall was empty, but the lights were on in the sitting room. Lisa was standing before the ashes of the log fire, hunched into a white furry jacket, her pale hair done up in an intricate fashion. She looked frail and very beautiful.

Emma ran across the room to her. 'Lisa—darling, how lovely! I've only been back a few hours—I was going to come along and see you tomorrow. How are you, and how's everything?' She put her arms round her young cousin and hugged her warmly.

Lisa drew away. 'I rang Daddy a little while ago. He said you'd just come back home—with Trent Marston.' Her pretty lips curled over his name contemptuously. 'So much for your promise not to have anything to do with him. You went straight off to Mexico with him, didn't you? I do hope he gave you a good time.'

Emma took her hand and drew her towards the sofa. 'Darling, come and sit down and relax. It wasn't like that. I had to go to Mexico because of Joe, and Trent had to come because of the firm's business there. So of course we were together there.'

Lisa's face was stony. 'Daddy says you're going to marry him. I told him he must be mistaken, but he stuck to it. That's why I've come here now, to see you. You're not going to marry him, are you, Emma? You know the way he treated me—you couldn't marry him after that, could you?'

'Why not?' Emma said quietly. She was trying to keep this on a reasonable level. She knew of old how easily Lisa could get upset. 'I know what you think of him, but it would be me who was taking the risk, not you.' She put an arm round Lisa and felt the slight body tremble under the soft white fur of her jacket. 'Darling, I know you believe he treated you badly, and I'm sorry about that, but men are men and they don't look at things the same way that we do.'

'You can say that again!' Lisa bit the words out between her small, even teeth. 'He's conned you too, hasn't he, and you've fallen for it. I told you it would happen, but you wouldn't listen.' She stood up and began pacing nervously about the room. 'He's a swine, that man—a callous—disgusting——' The words poured out, words that Emma wouldn't have believed Lisa knew.

At last she came to a halt, looking down at Emma, her face white, intense. 'You *can't* marry him. If you love me—if you've ever loved me—you can't do this to me!'

Emma frowned. Surely Lisa wasn't just acting up? Surely she had grown out of her fantasies now she was a married woman? What she had felt for Trent must have gone very deep, deeper than Emma had suspected. Gently she said, 'I'm sorry, Lisa darling, I do love you, but I love Trent too, and I'm going to marry him.'

Lisa stumbled backwards as if she had received a physical blow. 'Then I'll have to tell you. I wasn't going to, but now I'll have to.'

Something she saw in Lisa's face made Emma feel icy cold. 'Tell me—what?'

Lisa's pretty mouth hardened. 'Why do you think I married Richard all of a sudden?' The words came tumbling out in a high, agitated rush. 'I was pregnant when we were married. I should think the baby will be about a month too early.' She stopped and added slowly, significantly, 'And whose baby do you think it is?'

There was a long silence. Somewhere out in the garden a night bird called, a high wailing cry. Emma stared ahead, seeing nothing. Her skin was crawling cold, her mouth was dry. 'No,' she muttered at last through stiff lips. 'No—no—no——'

'Yes,' said Lisa, nodding her head up and down.

'Does—does Richard know?'

'Of course he does.'

'And he doesn't mind?'

'Richard would have taken me at any price.' Lisa touched her hair, smoothing it back, and for one pathetic moment she was the old Lisa, sure of her charm, her ability to get anything she wanted.

She sank down on the sofa beside Emma and grasped her hand. 'You won't tell anyone, will you, Emma?' Her great blue eyes were pleading. 'It would be awful if it got around—you know how gossipy small towns are. And Richard's mother would take it very badly. Richard's mother thinks I'm wonderful,' she added with a twisted little smile.

Emma felt nothing. The pain would come later. It was like a mortal wound—you didn't feel the sword-thrust into your heart at first.

Lisa bit her lip, and her eyes were swimming with tears. 'I'm sorry, Emma darling, I didn't want to hurt you. But you see, I had to tell you. I couldn't let you go on, not knowing. You can't marry him now, can you?'

Emma stood up stiffly. She felt like a very, very old woman, with nothing more to expect of life. 'I shouldn't think so,' she said.

She saw the quick relief on her cousin's face. Relief and—was it a touch of triumph, too? She supposed she couldn't begrudge Lisa that, after all she had suffered. 'I think you'd better go now, Lisa,' she said. 'I'm rather tired.'

Lisa put her arms round her and kissed her and the soft white, perfumed fur brushed Emma's cheek. 'I'm sorry, Em,' she said again, and went out to her waiting car.

Somehow Emma got through the night. If she could have cried it might have been a relief, but she was beyond tears. She felt drained, empty, like a dried-up river-bed when the river has changed its course and flowed elsewhere. At some time, sitting by the window, staring out at the darkened garden, she realised that her teeth were chattering and she got up and switched on the electric fire and wrapped herself in a dressing-gown. But she couldn't make herself get into bed.

As soon as it was light she pulled off the clothes she was wearing and got into a hot bath. It wouldn't do to get a chill; that would complicate everything. She got into trousers and a warm sweater, but she was still cold all through.

The house began to stir early. She heard Jessie go downstairs, and, later, Uncle Edward's firm tread along the landing. After a few minutes she joined him in the breakfast room.

He beamed affectionately at her. 'Good morning, Emma, you're an early bird. I thought you'd sleep off your jet-lag this morning.'

She poured herself coffee. 'I don't get jet-lag,' she said, with a small, brittle laugh. Only heartbreak, and you can't sleep that off.

She waited until Uncle Edward had almost finished his breakfast. Then she said brightly, 'About my going to Germany for another year—you know, we discussed it before.'

'Did we?' He looked puzzled.

'Oh yes, don't you remember? I've been thinking a lot about it while I've been away, and I do feel that if it's all right with you it would be better for me to leave Trent to get on with organising the new company here, for the time being.' The ordinariness of her own voice surprised her.

Uncle Edward frowned. 'But I thought——' He looked keenly into her face. Then he sighed. 'Oh well, if you're quite sure that's what you really want——'

'I am,' she said firmly.

Uncle Edward didn't often look cross, but at this moment he did. 'Then you'd better get in touch with the folk you stayed with before and see what you can fix up,' he said gruffly. And still frowning, he went off to his workroom, leaving a whole cup of coffee untouched on the table.

Somehow Emma got through the morning. She helped Jessie with the cleaning, polishing tables and chairs until her arm ached and Jessie began to look suspiciously at her. After that she walked up to the headland beside the house, where there was only the odd hiker, and the sea-birds, and a few cows. The headland had always been a favourite place of Emma's and she had walked here for miles over the soft turf, with the breeze on her cheeks, watching the white, ragged cliffs below with the waves foaming and beating round them. But today she saw nothing. She plodded on, looking straight ahead, taking the familiar route that led through the wood and down to the road. The July sun was hot on her face, but she felt cold, right through to her bones.

Meet me at the office at one, Trent had said. At midday Emma changed into a green linen shirtwaister dress, got out her Mini, and drove across the car-ferry and along the familiar road to Poole.

There was a parking space at the front of the office and she stopped the car and got out. Here was Trent's big surprise, then. The whole premises had acquired a fresh new look. The café had gone, and once more the frontage was joined into one—spruced up, repainted, and with a shiny bronze plate on the door, reading:

Fairley Brothers and Marston
Navigational Instruments

Like a girl in a trance, Emma slid open the heavy
door and went inside. Here the same magic had been
at work. The small, cramped area had become large
and spacious again, as it had been once before, when
shiny new boats stood here.

The work-force, too, had apparently expanded.
There were about twenty girls busy at their tables. A
tall man whom she hadn't seen before was strolling
round overseeing. Surely Trent hadn't got rid of Ted
Draper? But even as the thought surfaced, Ted himself
came through the door from the office—a different
Ted, in a neat navy-blue suit and blue collar, his tow-
coloured hair brushed back slickly.

He walked up to her, smiling all over his face. 'Well,
Miss Emma, what about this, then? A bit of a change,
isn't it?'

'It is indeed,' Emma said weakly. 'A change for the
better, I'm sure.'

'You're dead right,' Ted told her. 'Better for me,
that's for sure, to say nothing of the wife and kids.
You're looking at the new Production Manager, Miss
Emma.'

Emma shook hands and congratulated him warmly.
She went round and spoke to the girls she knew, and
everywhere it was the same story, the same satisfied
grin. Oh yes, Trent Marston had worked a miracle, all
right. Suddenly Emma was conscious of a fierce desire
to be part of the miracle, to share the satisfaction with
him, the success that was always waiting for a man like
Trent.

She thrust away the thought. There was no way that
could happen now.

She walked slowly through the door into the office.
A new-look office it was, of course. She might have
expected that Trent wouldn't be satisfied with the old,

somewhat cramped quarters. There was a corridor now, with light wooden doors leading off.

Rose, the secretary, appeared to have three girls working under her instead of one. There was a shiny new electric typewriter on her desk and two phones, as well as an intercom. She seemed to be very busy, but spared a moment to greet Emma, in a slightly self-important voice.

'This is all so new to me,' said Emma. 'Which is Mr Marston's office, Rose?'

She was conducted to a newly-furnished office at the far end of the corridor. 'I'm expecting Mr Marston back at one,' Rose told her, in her new, secretarial voice. 'Can I get you anything, Miss Fairley? A cup of coffee?'

'No, thank you, Rose, I'll just wait here for him.'

She sat down rather quickly in a comfortable leather chair, as her knees were feeling like stretched elastic. Rose hovered for a moment, nodded and went out, closing the door behind her.

Presently Emma heard a car draw up outside and recognised the sound of the engine. She heard Trent's voice as soon as he came into the office. She knew his step in the corridor, she would have known his step from any other in the whole world, she thought numbly. There was an awful lot she would have to forget, very soon.

He threw open the door and kicked it closed behind him. In a couple of steps he was standing in front of her, bending over her, pulling her up into his arms, his dark eyes brilliant.

She struggled away, pushing at his chest with both hands.

'It's all right, Emma, we're quite alone,' he chuckled. 'Sweetheart, I couldn't wait to get back to you. I've——' He paused. 'Emma? Is something the matter? You're not ill, are you?' His face was suddenly anxious.

She gathered all her strength and moved away from him, round to the other side of the desk. She met his troubled gaze and, drawing a quick breath, said flatly, 'Lisa came to see me last night, after you'd left.'

'Oh yes?' He eyed her—warily, she thought.

'She came to tell me she's pregnant.'

He actually smiled. 'Well, good for her. They should be——'

'Trent——' she broke in, in an odd, strangled voice. 'You don't understand. She was in a terrible state. Uncle Edward had told her he thought that you and I—that we were——' She choked on the words.

'Now look, darling,' said Trent with a touch of impatience, 'don't you think we've had enough of Lisa and her dramatics? Can't we give it a rest?'

Emma could hardly believe her ears. Was he going to bluff it out—pretend he didn't know anything about it? She looked at him as if he were a stranger. 'She told me that the baby is yours.'

There was a long, frozen silence in the office. From the next room came the busy clack of a typewriter, the buzz of a telephone, but in here it was as if life were suspended, waiting.

At last Trent spoke. He said very quietly, 'You thought I was the kind of man who'd get a girl pregnant and then walk out on her? You thought she'd married Richard as a cover-up. The faithful boy-next-door, ready to step into the breach?'

She gazed dumbly at him. The iciness of his voice, the hardness of his face, terrified her.

'And what about Richard?' he went on. 'Is he supposed to know about all this?'

Suddenly it was too much. 'Stop it——!' she cried, putting her hands over her ears. 'I didn't think about all that—I couldn't. I only thought that every time I looked at Lisa's baby I would—would see——' She sank down into a chair, her knees trembling violently.

Trent threw her a contemptuous look. 'A very pretty

picture!' He bit out the words as if they were poison.
Then he turned his back on her and walked across to
the window and stood there, stiff and unyielding.

It took all Emma's strength to speak to that tall, rigid
back, but somehow she forced the words out. 'Trent,
try to understand. I've loved Lisa all my life. She's
been as dear as a younger sister to me. We've shared
everything, told each other everything. I couldn't
just——' Tears flooded into her eyes. She leant her
forehead on the desk, while the tears rolled slowly
down her cheeks.

He turned round but did not come nearer. He said
slowly, 'Emma, I've always told you the truth, although you haven't always believed me. I'm telling you
the plain truth now when I say that Lisa's baby isn't
mine, whatever she may have said to you. It couldn't
possibly be, for the simple reason that we never slept
together.'

Her head shot up. This was something she hadn't
considered. 'Then why did she——'

'Look, Emma,' he cut in, and now his voice wasn't
accusing, it was stern and quiet. 'This is where you
have to make a choice. You have to decide who you're
going to believe, Lisa or me. It's as basic as that. I
can't offer you any proof—only my word. It's up to
you to think about it and make up your mind.' He
walked to the door and stood there. His face was haggard, the features looked as the graven features of one
of his Spanish ancestors must have looked. 'Only for
God's sake don't take too long about it, will you?'

She was on her feet in a second. He was going—
leaving her—and she didn't have to think it out. She
acted instinctively, without thinking or willing.
'Trent—don't go——' The words seemed to come
from deep inside her somewhere.

He turned but kept one hand on the door. 'There's
no more to say.' He bit out the words curtly.
'Arguments won't help.'

She stumbled blindly towards him, holding out her hands. 'But I don't *want* to argue, Trent. I only want to say that I believe you. Of course I believe you—I love you.'

For a moment he stood very still, staring incredulously at her, the muscles in his strong face working, and she thought he was near to tears himself. Then she was in his arms and they were clinging together, and her face was pressed hard against his, the taste of salt on her lips.

In the next office the telephone buzzed again. 'Come on,' said Trent, 'let's get out of here. Fairley Brothers and Marston can manage to get along without us for a while.'

He gripped her hand and they ran along the corridor and out through the side door and on to the quay, like two children let out of school. The breeze met them and Emma threw back her head and laughed, in a kind of frenzy of joy, and relief from unbearable tension. Her hair was blown into a tangle and she put up her hands to it with a little squeal.

Trent bent and kissed her swiftly. 'We'll walk,' he said, and there was new energy in his voice and a kind of triumph. 'I'm going to find the best jeweller in the town and put a ring on your finger, so everyone will know you're my woman,'

They walked together, arms entwined, along the old quay towards the town. It was the height of the season and the harbour was dotted thickly with sails, white and red and brown. Emma had always loved days like this, when the breeze came strongly off the sea, but now the sunshine had a new brilliance, the choppy water a deeper blue, because Trent was beside her and everything was right between them. She didn't have to doubt him any more—she just *knew*.

They chose a shop in the town centre, and when the assistant had taken one look at Trent and discovered what he wanted, they were ushered into a back room, evidently reserved for important customers, and the manager himself arrived to set before them the velvet-lined cases of rings that flashed and glittered in the electric lighting. Emma was speechless as she tried on one after the other of the beautiful things—diamonds, sapphires, emeralds—single stones, bars, clusters, modern designs. They all looked fabulously expensive and she glanced at Trent questioningly, but he sat back in his chair, smiling, obviously unconcerned about the price.

Finally she chose a single emerald in a filigree setting of pure white gold. When the manager had gone out of the room to phone for confirmation of the cheque, Trent took the ring from its tiny case and slipped it on to Emma's finger. 'I just want to see it there,' he said softly, lifting her hand and pressing his lips against it.

Emma was living in a rainbow dream. This was the most wonderful moment of her life and she wanted it to last on and on, for ever. She smiled mistily up at Trent and held his hand against her cheek.

They came out into the sunny street again. 'Now what?' said Trent. 'I think a celebration is in order. Have you lunched? No? Then I suggest we make for that restaurant where we lunched together that first time. We'll plight our eternal troth in champagne.' He grinned down at her and squeezed her arm hard. Emma was feeling decidedly lightheaded already and she daren't think what champagne was going to do to her. In her present mood it didn't seem to matter very much.

But as they came into the small bar of the Golden Butterfly sober reality returned instantly and she gripped Trent's arm. 'Look,' she hissed. 'Over there, by the bar. Richard.'

Trent was unperturbed. 'So?' There was a faint smile on his face as he followed her gaze. 'The moment of truth is upon us.'

Richard had seen them. He slipped off his high stool

and came towards them, beaming expansively and shaking them both by the hand. He was, Emma saw at once, rather more than half-way towards being drunk. His face was pink and shiny, under the thatch of flaming red hair and his blue eyes were having a certain difficulty in focussing.

'Business lunch,' he explained carefully, as they all sat down at the nearest table. 'Couple of fellows from London—just left. Well, how's life, Emma? I hear you've been swanning round Mexico.' He looked at Trent in a puzzled kind of way, as if he couldn't quite place him.

'You met Trent at the wedding,' Emma said. 'He's coming into the firm.'

'Ah yes, of course, jolly good, jolly good!' He shook Trent's hand heartily once again.

Trent said smoothly, 'We hear we have to congratulate you and Lisa. Are you pleased?'

Richard's face went even pinker and assumed the smug satisfaction of the father-to-be. 'Stunning, isn't it? It takes a bit of getting used to—me, a father!' He giggled foolishly. 'But we're all very bucked. Mother can't wait to be a granny.'

'When's the infant arriving?' Trent asked casually.

Richard's face became suddenly rueful and confidential. He leaned across the table and spoke in an undertone. 'Strictly between ourselves—round about November. Rather naughty, I'm afraid. It'll set the local ladies counting on their fingers. But when Lisa finally decided to have me I'm afraid we both got a bit carried away. You know how it is?' He looked towards Trent for a man-to-man confirmation, and Trent grinned back and said, 'Sure. Sure,' in comfortable understanding.

'We'll have another drink on it,' Richard said, and began to struggle to his feet, but Trent was up first.

'Mine, I think. We have something to celebrate too, haven't we, Emma?'

He touched her left hand and Richard goggled at the emerald glittering there.

'Well, blow me down! Golly, this is a fair corker! Does Lisa know? She'll be chuffed to bits when I tell her.'

Emma's eyes sought Trent's and saw the amused gleam in them. What had so nearly been a tragedy was turning into a farce.

Trent bought drinks and it was all very friendly and jolly. By the time Richard left them, with more fulsome congratulations on all sides, Emma was beginning to feel as if she were floating inches above the ground.

Trent turned to her with his enigmatic smile, only now it didn't anger or confuse her. She felt that at last she was beginning to understand something of this man she loved. 'Well,' he said, 'was that proof enough for you?'

She pulled a face at him. 'I didn't need proof.'

'No, I know you didn't, bless you,' he said, very low, 'and I'll always remember that, my darling.'

Afterwards, the one thing that Emma managed to recall about the lunch that followed was the roast duckling. It was probably delicious, but she hardly tasted it. She watched the bubbles rising in her champagne glass and felt as light as a bubble herself.

They walked back to the office and picked up Trent's car. 'We'll make for home and tell them our news,' he said. 'But we'll go the long way round.'

They took the road that crossed the heath and after a mile or so they got out of the car and walked a little way along a narrow, rough path. There was nobody in sight, and no sound except for the chirping of grasshoppers and the carolling of larks high overhead. Most of the gorse was over now, but here and there little bursts of gold showed between the tufts of heather and grass. It was very peaceful.

Trent's arm was close about Emma. She looked up at him, frowning slightly, and said, 'Why do you think

Lisa should want to do that to me, Trent?'

His own thoughts must have been miles away, because it was a full minute before he replied. 'Because, my love, Lisa is a spoilt child still—a child living in a fantasy world. She thinks she should be able to get anything she happens to want, and if she doesn't get it she'll do everything she can to make sure that nobody else does. Least of all, you.' He smiled down at her tenderly. 'You, who—if I can believe what Edward tells me—have done quite a bit of the spoiling.'

She thought for a while and then sighed. 'Yes, I suppose that's true. Do you think she'll grow up—when she has her own child, perhaps?'

He shrugged. 'Who can tell? But do we have to go on talking about Lisa? She doesn't really matter, she could never have hurt us in the long run, my darling girl, we've got too much going for us.'

He stopped and pulled her down beside him in a hollow of dried grass and took her face in both his hands, his dark eyes gazing into hers as if he could never get enough of what he saw there. 'I adore you, Emma,' he whispered huskily. 'I never thought I should find a girl like you. You're the most wonderful thing that ever happened to me.'

'And yet you went away and left me for weeks.'

'That was pure hell,' he muttered, 'but it had to be done. You kept on saying you hated me.'

'I had to keep on saying it,' she confessed, 'in case I told you I was falling fathoms deep in love with you. I think you bewitched me, but I never imagined you were serious about me.'

He groaned. 'Serious! I was besotted. I put poor Juanita through the third degree on the phone, to find out if there was any bloke out there trying anything on with you.'

She said demurely, 'There was Luis Valesco. He——'

'*What?*' he roared, sitting up straight.

'He must have been around seventy,' she added, as if he hadn't interrupted.

He sank down beside her, pulling her roughly into his arms. 'Enough of this,' he said, and there was a touch of the old arrogant Trent in his voice now. 'You're my woman from now on, and I've waited too long already. When will you marry me?'

She pretended to consider, but the sight of his dark face so close above hers was making her heart plunge wildly.

'Let me see—how about tomorrow?'

He gave a shout of laughter and tightened his arms round her. 'I don't know if I can wait that long.'

His hands went to the front zip of her linen dress. The zip stuck half-way and with trembling hands she finished the job for him, everything in her aching for his kisses. She put her arms round his neck and drew his head down, shuddering with delight at the touch of his lips on her swelling breast.

His mouth inched its way up her neck as his hands began to move over her body, lovingly, caressingly. He kissed her chin and muttered thickly, 'But it's going to be worth waiting for, don't you think, my love?'

'Yes—oh yes!' His face above hers was blotting out the sun. She closed her eyes and the whole world was engulfed in a great wave of love and longing.

'*Yes*,' she managed to gasp again just before his lips closed over hers.

Harlequin Plus

A WORD ABOUT THE AUTHOR

Marjorie Lewty was born in Liverpool, where her mother managed a neighborhood movie theater. The old building became a second home to Marjorie, and she could often be found munching sandwiches while sitting in a tiny viewing room watching films featuring the great stars. "No wonder," she recalls, "I became a writer of romance."

After leaving school she worked in a Liverpool bank for ten years ("very unromantic," she says); then she met her husband-to-be, a young dental surgeon. Within a few months they were married—(very romantic, we believe).

Soon the Second World War broke out, and Marjorie, then, living in Birmingham, trained as an ambulance driver. It was at this point that she began to write. The timing might seem strange but, as Marjorie explains, "The important things in one's life happen because they have to happen. Something goes 'click' and the wheel of your life turns a fraction."

She heard that click when she saw an ad for a course in short-story writing. "And," she recalls happily, "an obsession began that has lasted ever since." From short stories she graduated to serials and eventually to novels. Her first Harlequin, *Alex Rayner, Dental Nurse* (Romance #953), was published in 1965.

Harlequin Presents...

**Stories to dream about...
Stories of love...**

...all-consuming, passionate love,
the way you've always imagined it,
the way you know it should be!

Harlequin Romances

The books that let you escape into the wonderful world of romance! Trips to exotic places...interesting plots...meeting memorable people... the excitement of love.... These are integral parts of Harlequin Romances – the heartwarming novels read by women everywhere.

Many early issues are now available. Choose from this great selection!

Choose from this list of
Harlequin Romance editions.*

Some of these book were originally published under different titles.

Relive a great love story...
with Harlequin Romances
Complete and mail this coupon today!

Harlequin Reader Service

In the U.S.A.
1440 South Priest Drive
Tempe, AZ 85281

In Canada
649 Ontario Street
Stratford, Ontario N5A 6W2

Please send me the following Harlequin Romance novels. I am enclosing my check or money order for $1.50 for each novel ordered, plus 75¢ to cover postage and handling.

☐ 982	☐ 1156	☐ 1180	☐ 1195	☐ 1221
☐ 984	☐ 1162	☐ 1181	☐ 1200	☐ 1222
☐ 1015	☐ 1168	☐ 1183	☐ 1203	☐ 1237
☐ 1048	☐ 1172	☐ 1184	☐ 1204	☐ 1238
☐ 1126	☐ 1173	☐ 1186	☐ 1214	☐ 1248
☐ 1151	☐ 1175	☐ 1187	☐ 1215	☐ 1314

Number of novels checked @ $1.50 each = $ _____

N.Y. and Ariz. residents add appropriate sales tax. $ _____

Postage and handling $ _____ .75

TOTAL $ _____

I enclose _____
(Please send check or money order. We cannot be responsible for cash ser
 through the mail.)

Prices subject to change without notice.

NAME _____
(Please Print)

ADDRESS _____
(APT. NO.)

CITY _____

STATE/PROV. _____

ZIP/POSTAL CODE _____

Offer expires March 31, 1983   2095600000